Jayden's Rescue

by Vladimir Tumanov

illustrated by David Bordeleau

D0167445

Scholastic Canada Ltd.
Toronto New York London Auckland Sydney
Mexico City New Delhi Hong Kong

Scholastic Canada Ltd.
175 Hillmount Road, Markham, Ontario L6C 1Z7, Canada

Scholastic Inc.
555 Broadway, New York, NY 10012, USA

Scholastic Australia Pty Limited
PO Box 579, Gosford, NSW 2250, Australia

Scholastic New Zealand Limited
Private Bag 94407, Greenmount, Auckland, New Zealand

Scholastic Ltd.
Villiers House, Clarendon Avenue, Leamington Spa,
Warwickshire CV32 5PR, UK

National Library of Canada Cataloguing in Publication Data

Tumanov, Vladimir A., 1961-
        Jayden's rescue

ISBN 0-439-98864-0

I. Title.

PS8589.U6067J39 2002   C813'.6   C2001-902736-2
PZ7.T8233Ja 2002

Edited by Laura Peetoom.

6 5 4 3 2   Printed in Canada   04 05 06

To Larissa, Alex, Vanessa . . . and Kayla

Chapter 1

The Find

Alex Isaac Fog was watching snowflakes land on his hand when, out of nowhere, something dropped near his feet.

He bent down. It was a pencil. At the same time, he heard footsteps, as if someone was walking by right next to him. The sound became fainter and then disappeared altogether. But there was no one around!

Alex picked up the pencil and examined it. Silver-coloured, and covered with little bright-blue numbers, it was longer and thicker than most. Instead of an eraser, the pencil had a tip shaped like a miniature castle.

Alex put the strange find into his pencil case. His hands trembled a little as he thought about the footsteps. But there was no time to investigate. The bus had arrived.

Alex climbed in and plunked himself down next to his best friend, Sam. Sam was in Alex's grade but in Mr. Cohen's class. They always sat together on the way to and from school.

It was Monday morning, and that meant only one thing to Alex: a math test. Alex's teacher Ms Lund loved to say, "You need to wake up your brain cells at the start of a week!" As far as Alex was concerned, it was more like *fry* your brain cells. At the start of a math test, Alex's brain would seize up and stay that way until he heard those unavoidable words: "Turn in your papers, please." And he wasn't proud of what he turned in, time after time. There were no surprises for Alex. He was lucky if Ms Lund gave him the occasional C.

Alex tried, he really did. He excelled at all his other subjects, especially language arts. His essays and stories won prizes in school contests and even city-wide competitions. But what Alex loved most was reading. If he was nowhere to be seen, everyone in the family knew that he was probably in some cozy corner of the house, hunched over a book. Fantasy was his favourite. Alex had read all the books on his bookshelves and checked a huge pile out of the library each month.

But whenever he had to review for a math test or finish a math assignment, the same thing would happen. After a few minutes of staring blankly at the numbers, Alex's hands would creep over to his current book and soon, as if by magic, he'd be transported somewhere else, battling sorcerers by the castleful using an array of magic spells. In no time at all, it would be ten o'clock and time for bed. Too bad, no time left for math. Maybe tomorrow.

Well, tomorrow was here: Monday, the day when all wizards and dungeons magically vanished, leaving a dust storm of plus and minus signs behind. Alex's thoughts drifted to the book he'd been reading last night. It was about a boy who discovers he is a wizard. Alex wished he could become a wizard – then he could put a spell on Ms Lund to make her forget about tests. But Alex wasn't a wizard, or even a wizard's apprentice. He was just an ordinary kid, going to an ordinary school.

Wait a minute – not quite ordinary. Alex elbowed Sam in the ribs and pulled out the new pencil.

"Look what I found," he said.

"Awesome," replied Sam. "You want to trade? I'll give you a pen that writes in four colours, and I've got this – "

"Forget it! This thing is way too cool." Alex looked at it again closely and then put it back into his pencil case. "I'll use it on my math test today. Maybe it'll bring me luck. I could use some."

Sam shrugged his shoulders and looked out the window.

For a moment Alex thought of telling Sam about the footsteps, but then he changed his mind. Sam would never believe it. He wanted proof for everything. He had no patience for Alex's fantasy novels. The books that Sam read were about bugs, engines, oceans and space. "Real stuff," as he said. Sam's best subject in school was science.

At school, Alex hurried to his locker, put his coat away, grabbed his backpack and went straight to class. Lots of other kids were already there, gossiping and goofing around. "What are they so cheerful about?" Alex grumbled to himself.

The bell rang. The sound was unpleasantly shrill and made Alex cringe. Ms Lund said in her usual calm way, "Settle down, please. Put away all books and take out one pencil. You may begin as soon as you receive the test." Then she handed out the papers. Alex reached into his pencil case and took out the new pencil. Once more he looked at the castle and the blue numbers. His stomach was now a tense, gurgling knot.

As he began to read the first question, the usual panic gripped him:

An ant is sitting at one end of a long twig. Suddenly, it notices a friend at the other end and decides to go for a visit. The ant begins to move at a speed of 2 centimetres per second. It takes the ant 7 seconds to reach the friend. How long is the twig?

Alex didn't know where to start, but he couldn't just sit there without writing anything. He touched the paper with the pencil, and an incredible thing happened: the pencil began to pull on his hand! Half terrified and half thrilled, Alex just watched – his moving hand no longer belonged to him. Before he knew it, the solution was written down:

If it takes the ant 7 seconds to go from one end of the twig to the other, that time has to be multiplied by the distance per second (2 centimetres). 7 × 2 = 14. The twig is 14 centimetres long.

Alex had no time to wonder. The pencil kept moving, solving problem after problem. Just to see what would happen, Alex looked away for a moment. The pencil continued writing, and never stopped until the test was finished. Bewildered, Alex stood, with quivering knees, and handed in his paper. He was the first one done!

Laura, the class math champion, looked suspiciously at Alex as he took his seat again. He could just imagine what she was thinking: Alex Fog couldn't have finished the test! He must have given up! Ms Lund cast a doubtful glance at his paper, but her expression quickly turned to surprise when she saw his scribbled answers. She looked up and gave Alex an encouraging grin.

At lunch, Alex flew to Sam's table and started talking faster than he could think. "I have proof! I have proof! The pencil is magic! It's magic! And I know because it just – "

"What are you talking about? What pencil?" asked Sam. He put down his half-eaten salami sandwich.

As Alex gave his account of the math test, Sam stared at him, as if trying to figure out the joke. Then he started to smirk. "Your *pencil* wrote the math test for you . . . ?"

It was obvious he didn't believe a word Alex was saying. A moment of tense silence followed, as Alex desperately searched for a way of convincing Sam. And suddenly it came to him.

"See those older kids over there?" he said, pointing to a nearby table. "Follow me, and I'll give you so much proof, it'll be coming out your ears."

Reluctantly, Sam followed Alex. When the upper-grade girls crowded around the table saw the two boys, their conversation stopped in mid-sentence. They stared curiously at the visitors.

Alex gulped, cleared his throat and blurted out: "Hi. Could you do us a favour, please? Does anyone have a math textbook I could borrow for a second?"

One of the girls did have one, and she handed it over with an amused smile. Back at their table, Alex and Sam sat down, opened the book and found the hardest-looking problem. Even Sam, who was pretty good at math, couldn't figure it out.

A truck sets out from town A at a speed of 45 kilometres per hour toward town B. Another truck sets out from town B for town A at a speed of 54 kilometres per hour. They meet 20 minutes later. What is the distance between towns A and B?

Alex took out the pencil and a piece of paper. As Sam watched, the pencil began to write so quickly, it looked like Alex knew it all by heart. In no time at all, the answer was there:

20 minutes goes into 60 minutes 3 times, so 20 minutes is 1/3 of an hour. To find out how far the 1st truck goes in 20 minutes, find out 1/3 of 45 kilometres per hour. 45 ÷ 3 = 15 kilometres. The first truck has covered 15 kilometres of the way from town A toward town B in 20 minutes. The same is done for the second truck. 54 ÷ 3 = 18. In 20 minutes the second truck has gone 18

kilometres. So when the first truck is 15 kilometres away from town A on the way to town B, and the second truck is 18 kilometres away from town B on the way to town A, they meet. Add up the two distances: 15 + 18 = 33. The towns are 33 kilometres apart.

Before he looked up at Sam, Alex knew exactly what his friend's expression would be. Sam was paler than the sheet of paper in his hand. He stared, first at the solution, then at Alex, in utter bewilderment. Then Sam himself picked up the pencil, turned to another problem in the book and watched his own hand race across the paper. The solution materialized out of nowhere.

There was a long silence. Finally, Sam croaked, "This is so freaky, it scares me!"

"You've got to be kidding! What's there to be scared of? It's just like in all my books!" But he had to admit, it *was* pretty freaky.

"Sorry for not believing you earlier," gulped Sam, then quickly added, "I think we should keep this to ourselves. If anyone in the school found out about – "

Before Sam could get the words out, the boys heard a hesitant voice: "Can I try it too? . . . I promise I won't tell."

Chapter 2

The Threesome

Alex and Sam swung around. Standing right behind them was Vanessa. She was in their grade, but Alex and Sam didn't talk to her much. Alex felt sorry about this sometimes. Vanessa was one of the nicest people he knew. She could always come up with a serene kind of smile, no matter what others said or did. Like the way she was smiling now. Alex couldn't help smiling back.

"You two don't know how to keep secrets very well," Vanessa continued. Curiosity was written all over her face, but she was obviously trying to play it cool. "Next time, keep it quiet if you don't want others to hear you."

"So you've heard everything we've said?" said Sam, and exchanged a secretive glance with Alex.

"Most of it, but I swear I won't tell a soul! So please, can I have a turn?" Vanessa moved a strand of wavy dark hair off her cheek and hesitantly held out an upturned palm.

Alex sighed and dropped the pencil into her hands. "Okay, you're in. But you're the last one to know. Swear!"

"My lips are sealed. Cross my heart," muttered Vanessa as she hurriedly took out a small notepad. She found a tough problem to try, and the pencil leaped into action.

"Wow!" she cried. Her eyes were sparkling with excitement. "Let's try some more!"

Sam and Vanessa took turns solving problem after problem, until Alex stopped them.

"There's one more thing you should know, guys," he said, very seriously. "When I found the pencil at the bus stop, I could hear someone's footsteps . . . but there was *no one there.*"

There was silence for a moment. Then, "Who cares?" chirped Vanessa, barely keeping still on her seat. "Wherever it came from, this pencil is fantastic!"

"You must have imagined the footsteps," Sam assured Alex. "The main thing is that the pencil's ours now. Can you picture what we can do with it?"

* * *

In a few days, Ms Lund handed back the math tests.

"Chi, Laura Elizabeth; Descartes, Renée Claude; . . . " Ms Lund had a thing for using people's full names. Taking attendance in the morning lasted forever.

" . . . Fog, Alex Isaac . . . " When his name was called, Alex strolled confidently to the teacher's desk.

"Good work, Alex!" said Ms Lund. "I knew you had it in you. Keep it up."

Back at his desk, Alex looked at his mark . . . and beamed. A+! The ant had made it to the other end of the fourteen-centimetre twig, and the other answers were right, too. But this was just the start. With the magic pencil, Alex would never dread Mondays again!

The three friends were soon having the time of their lives. They would go to the library, take out the hardest math books ever written and let the pencil do the work. Watching the incredible solutions take shape before their eyes, they hardly noticed the time pass.

One Monday morning, Alex noticed just how much shorter the pencil had become. It might have been magical, but it still needed sharpening. It had already shrunk to about two thirds of its original length.

Alex didn't know what to do. To Sam and Vanessa, the pencil was a cool toy. But this was no mere game for Alex – he depended on the pencil for all his math homework and tests, and he needed it to last at least until the end of the school year. His parents had promised that if he kept his math grades up until then, he would be allowed to go to Camp Waconda, which he'd been begging to do for ages. But at the rate they were going, the pencil wouldn't last more than another month.

Alex couldn't afford to let the pencil be whittled away just for fun, no matter how selfish it seemed to keep it to himself. Who was the real owner of the pencil, anyway? Who had found it in the first place? It wasn't Sam or Vanessa. Alex would have to talk to them.

The next day on the bus, Alex sat down with his friends and opened his mouth to say that the fun with the pencil would have to stop. But something entirely different came out.

"I've lost the pencil."

He hadn't meant to lie! But now it was too late, and . . . *maybe* it was for the best. This way, no feelings would get hurt.

Sam looked dismayed. "Are you serious? You've really lost it?"

"I've looked in my pockets, in my knapsack, in my desk . . . " Alex stared at the floor. "Sorry."

"Well, it wasn't going to last forever, anyway," Vanessa said in her usual cheery voice. "It would have shrunk to nothing sooner or later." She didn't sound at all disappointed.

Sam was, though. "That pencil was the most incredible thing we had!" he complained.

"*We* had? It was *my* pencil. I found it," replied Alex with a quivering voice.

There was a moment of silence. "And now you've lost it, have you?" Sam said, staring Alex straight in the eye. Then he turned his head and stared out the window. When the bus pulled into the school parking lot, Sam was the first person out the door.

Alex spent the rest of the week wandering around the school in a daze, avoiding even Vanessa's company. He felt truly ashamed of lying to his friends. Over the weekend, he made up his mind that he would tell the truth to them and apologize. Enough was enough. He would do it on Monday. At lunch.

On Monday morning, Alex opened his locker and reached into the secret hiding place where he always kept the magic pencil.

It was gone!

Shocked, Alex searched every corner of the locker, shaking out all his clothes, his lunchbox and even his gym things. The pencil was definitely gone.

Alex wrote the test as best he could, but he knew that without magic, he'd be back to failing grades. He gave up on his idea of the lunchtime apology. He felt too gloomy to talk to anyone.

At home, after barely touching his supper and complaining of a headache, Alex went to his room and shut the door. He had done a horrible thing to his friends and lost his magic pencil, all in one week. What was going to happen next?

Alex went to his bookshelf. Today, more than ever, he needed a good story to occupy his thoughts. *The Lion, the Witch and the Wardrobe? The Princess and the Goblin?* . . . hmm . . . *The Sword in the Stone?* . . . *The Neverending Story?*

As he tried to decide what to read, he suddenly noticed something strange. It was a book he had never seen before. How could that be? He knew his books inside out; he'd read every one of them more than once. Maybe it was a library book that he had forgotten to return – but no, there was no cataloguing information on the spine.

Alex pulled the book off the shelf and examined it. The top half of the front cover bore a picture of a silver castle, and below it was another illustration: a partly open wooden door, with dim light shining inside the doorway. *Jayden's*

Rescue, read the title, which sounded intriguing.

Alex had a strange feeling about the book – as if he had seen it, or something like it, before. Perhaps he'd read another book by the same author?

But there was no author listed anywhere on the spine, cover or title page. How strange! A little chill ran down Alex's spine as he turned to the first page.

Chapter 3

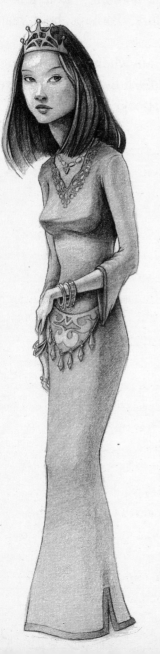

Jayden's Rescue

There was once a very happy and prosperous kingdom called Idyllia. It was ruled by a young queen named Jayden. She was tall and graceful, with flowing red hair and deep green eyes. To match her striking eyes, Jayden usually wore clothes of green, and so she was known as "The Emerald Queen." And it was a doubly fitting name, since Idyllia was well known for its lush groves and hills, towering cedars and rich meadows.

In addition to her beauty, the Emerald Queen's wisdom and fairness were legendary. Other rulers looked upon their kingdoms — and their people — as their property, and ruled accordingly. Jayden, however, always considered the welfare of her people first when making any important decision.

Jayden's parents had lost

their lives when she was but a child. And so, she and her younger sister Kira were brought up by the servants and courtiers of the royal household. From the earliest days the sisters were educated by an army of teachers in every known art and science. And by the time Jayden and Kira were fully grown women, they knew practically all there was to know, and perhaps even a little more.

It is therefore no wonder that under Jayden's rule, learning and creativity flourished at court and throughout the kingdom. Observatories were built on the highest mountains to track the movement of stars and planets. Painters and sculptors filled public spaces with their creations. Poets recited their works in special halls built just for that purpose in every town and city. Theatres offered free admission to plays for all ages and tastes. An annual prize for the best play was awarded by the queen herself, and in June, on the night of the summer solstice, the prize-winning play was performed for all on the grounds of the royal castle.

The Emerald Queen had schools built all over Idyllia, and made sure that every child had a chance to study. Teaching was one of the most respected professions, and Jayden paid her hundreds of teachers handsome salaries. But Jayden's involvement did not stop there: she was an esteemed teacher herself.

Children were always welcome in Jayden's castle. She taught them science and history, carpentry and geography, music and architecture. While there was nothing that did not interest this most admirable queen, Jayden's favourite subject was mathematics. No one in the land could explain the trickiest geometry theorems or most complicated algebra equations better than she did. If the kingdom's greatest mathematicians were stumped by some difficult problem, they inevitably presented themselves at the royal castle.

In her spare time Jayden wrote books, which were carefully illustrated by her sister, Kira. Read by young and old alike, the books were famous not only in Idyllia, but in other lands, too. Some were full of exciting stories, while others examined plants and animals or explored the mechanisms of marvellous machines.

Jayden was also very skilled at preventing conflicts with neighbouring kingdoms. Wars had occasionally flared up around Idyllia in the past, but since Jayden's ascension to the throne, no one had ever threatened her realm. She had a gift for warding off claims made against Idyllia.

Every year, in order to ensure an enduring peace with her neighbours, Jayden would hold a ball for all the rulers of nearby lands. They would arrive with their retinues and feast for days. Beautiful music and elegant dancers would entertain in the great banquet hall amidst bubbling fountains and bouquets of sweet-smelling flowers. The food and drink served to the Emerald Queen's guests would leave them speechless, and many a servant was sent to the kitchen to inquire about the recipes used by the royal cooks. After such celebrations it never even occurred to other monarchs to harm their charming hostess or invade her dream-like domain.

But during one such joyous reception, a new king appeared with an entourage of fearsome-looking attendants. His name was Rechner, and he was the ruler of a realm called Lugubria. Until recently Lugubria had been ruled by Rechner's elder brother Nestor, but a few months earlier, Nestor had died under mysterious circumstances. Rechner was immediately proclaimed King of Lugubria.

The other monarchs knew of Rechner, but no one had yet seen him. His coronation had been private, and Rechner's answer to every invitation to neighbouring-state functions had been "unable to attend." Although there had been some rumours of suffering in the land of the Lugubrians, nothing was known for certain. Such rumours came to the surface whenever a new king or queen was pronounced, and these rarely proved to be true. The new king would be given the benefit of the doubt. So, when Rechner's party entered Jayden's banqueting hall, a murmur of curiosity rippled through the crowd.

At first the celebration went as brilliantly as always. There were mixed greens with duck confit and blackberries, roast pheasant with curried wild rice, and a dessert of caramel ice cream topped with passionfruit, cherries and grapes, served in bowls made of Turkish delight. The guests were enchanted.

For entertainment, in addition to the usual jugglers and acrobats, a number trickster commanded the room, offering to solve any multiplication or division problem instantly. Someone in the crowd would yell, "34,589,087 times 345,688!" and he would immediately cry out his answer.

Near the end of the evening, King Rechner abruptly rose to his feet. He raised a goblet of ruby wine, cleared his throat and, with an air of supreme confidence, spoke in such thunderous tones that the windows of the banqueting hall rattled with each word:

To you, fair queen, I raise my cup,
and to your sparkling eyes.
With you I've come to dance and sup,
For you are rich and wise.
And with this toast I would propose
to join our hearts and hands.
No one would ever dare oppose
the marriage of . . . our lands.

Everyone stopped talking at once, and all the guests stared
at Jayden. The Emerald Queen appeared to look inward at
first, clearly deep in thought. Then she stood up, smiled to her
guests and turned her eyes toward King Rechner.

You speak so well, oh mighty king;
I trust your words are pure.
But marriage is a tricky thing,
As you well know, I'm sure.
We've barely met; you seek my heart,
And with it, all my land.
This is, perhaps, our friendship's start;
for now, I'll shake your hand.

A scattering of applause was heard for Queen Jayden's
clever and diplomatic answer. But it died quickly as Rechner,
clearly unwilling to settle for a mere handshake of friendship,
threw his wine goblet to the floor. He glared one last time at
the dumbfounded crowd, his face twitching with anger. Then,
without uttering a sound, he stormed out of the hall. His
attendants followed close behind. It was a disturbing ending to

an otherwise superb feast, and more than one guest predicted no good would come of it.

Their predictions came true. Time passed, and Jayden continued teaching, writing and running the affairs of Idyllia. She heard no more from Rechner, and by the time she began planning her next feast she had quite forgotten about him. Rechner, however, had not forgotten her. One morning, as the court prepared to receive a group of ambassadors from a faraway land, Jayden's lady-in-waiting entered the royal bedchamber to wake Her Majesty and was stunned by what she saw. Furniture was overturned, windowpanes were shattered, there were books strewn all over the carpets. The Emerald Queen's bed was empty. On the wall above the dresser was scribbled the following message:

I proposed but she refused me — not a clever move.
Now I've taken what I wanted. Do you disapprove?
Tough! I say. She's mine. It's over. Jayden's gone for good.
Rechner takes what Rechner fancies. Is that understood?

Rechner, King of Lugubria

The whole castle was set into chaos. Jayden's sister Kira was notified, there was a meeting of the ministers, and the Idyllian generals were summoned. It was time to put Idyllia's idle army into action.

It was a heartbreaking day for Idyllia. Thousands of armed men marched along the kingdom's roads, gathering around the royal castle and dividing up into regiments under bright banners. Schools closed, and all the children were outside, watching the daunting spectacle of glistening armour and mighty steeds.

Finally, the army was on its way to Lugubria in full battle gear, with flags waving and trumpets blaring. However, after crossing the border, everyone was surprised to encounter no resistance. The Idyllian warriors travelled for days without lifting a single sword or shooting a single arrow.

But Rechner was prepared. Although the Idyllians did not know this yet, Rechner was no ordinary king. He was versed in black magic. His castle was full of books, but not the kinds of books that one would find in the many libraries of Jayden's kingdom. Rechner's books did not tell about shipbuilding or astronomy. They were full of spells and incantations, recipes for potions and poisons, astrological calculations and dark mysteries. So when the Idyllian army approached Rechner's stronghold, they found their way blocked, not by an opposing army, but by a huge wall of fire, several metres thick and tall. It rose up from the bare road, hot and crackling, seeming to feed on nothing but the air around it. A wonder like this had never been seen before.

At first the Idyllian generals gave the order to wait. All fires have to burn out sometime. But after hours of waiting everyone saw that the flames were not growing any weaker. All attempts to put the fire out with water caused it to grow and spread outward, threatening to engulf Jayden's would-be rescuers. For days the army stayed there, determined to save their queen, yet utterly helpless.

In the end, when the army's rations began to run out and the fire gave no signs of diminishing, the Idyllians had to admit defeat. They pulled up camp and reluctantly turned back toward their kingdom.

When the soldiers returned, everyone in Idyllia heard about the wall of fire and had to accept the loss of the Emerald Queen. The Idyllians were realistic: life had to continue; the kingdom needed a ruler. Therefore, soon Kira was crowned and set upon the throne. With a heavy heart, but determined to continue Jayden's good work, Kira did all that her older sister had done: the schools once again welcomed all children, scientists and artists were busy at work, and poetry was recited everywhere, though not quite as gladly as before.

And what of Jayden? Jayden had become a prisoner in Rechner's strange and foreboding castle. Building had begun just after the death of Rechner's brother and was completed in four short weeks. There was no doubt about Rechner's construction techniques. There was no discussion, either; strangely, all the workers who had participated in erecting the new king's castle vanished as soon as the last brick had been mortared.

The castle included twelve silver towers, some of which were so tall that they reached the clouds. Huge but empty halls, which stretched one after another almost without end, made up the royal quarters. There were very few windows in the walls, and Rechner did not like firelight. So the castle was cast in perpetual twilight, its inhabitants — mostly servants — roaming from room to room like ghosts. They huddled in tiny nooks inside the bottom part of each tower. They trembled at every noise — no one liked to be summoned by the castle's master. Those who displeased Rechner were punished with extreme cruelty.

Below ground there was a dungeon with four hundred

rooms, each one leading to the next. The sorcerer had ordered that Jayden be taken to the deepest cell, which was so remote that the outside world did not seem to exist for anyone unlucky enough to end up here. The room was lit by a weak oil lamp hanging from the ceiling. Spiders and centipedes crawled all over the walls.

As soon as Jayden had been untied and her blindfold taken off, she collapsed on the cold stone floor. Exhausted and terrified, Jayden expected no mercy from her captor. She worried about her kingdom, and hoped no one would waste time coming after her. She imagined that Rechner would make any kind of rescue impossible. She was almost right.

After a few minutes Jayden looked around the room, and, as her eyes grew used to the semi-darkness, she noticed two wooden doors: one in front of her and one behind. The door in front of her was slightly ajar, and a dim light came from the other side. Suddenly she heard the sound of a key turning in a lock. The door behind Jayden began to open very slowly. A broad figure stood at the threshold. Immediately Jayden recognized King Rechner himself.

The sorcerer took two steps toward Jayden, stopped and bowed to his prisoner. Then he began to speak in a sing-song voice:

> *In Rechner's dungeon you are stuck:*
> *four hundred rooms in all.*
> *(My castle is so very big,*
> *and you are rather small.)*
> *Two paths are open to you,*
> *two very different ways.*

One is to marry me at once,
and you'll see better days.
The other's hardly worth your time;
it is a quest so bleak,
so treacherous and difficult,
you won't find what you seek.
To leave your prison you must cross
each room: alas, poor lass!
At every door a monster stands
who will not let you pass
Unless you answer what he asks:
a riddle to decode.
The puzzles aim to twist your brain.
You'll crack under this load!
Solutions must be written down
and handed to my ghouls.
This is how my dungeon works;
King Rechner wrote the rules.
But if you see the light, my friend,
and wish to change your mind,
my heart, my throne, my crown are yours.
I can be very kind.

Jayden noticed a stack of paper in the corner of the room.
There were some pencils on top of it. Solving problems was
what she loved doing most, but Rechner obviously did not
know this. If the king was telling the truth, then, four hundred
rooms or four thousand, she would do her best to think her
way out of here!

She gave the sorcerer a look of disgust, making her choice

obvious. Rechner shrugged and turned around, looking back at Jayden once more before shutting and locking the door behind him. Immediately, the Emerald Queen went over to the stack of paper and picked up a handful of sheets, as well as a couple of pencils. There was no time to waste. She turned toward the other, partly open door. The streak of light that came through the crack was frightening and inviting at the same time. This door was her only choice. She walked up to it, and pulled the handle.

She shuddered at what she saw. Her path into the next room was blocked by a huge one-eyed monster. He was purple all over and had long green hair on his head. He had ten toes on each foot and ten fingers on each hand. The creature was holding a large metal staff with a knob that looked like an enormous diamond.

She closed her eyes for a moment and then opened them again. Although she considered it for a moment, Jayden did not turn back. She remained standing there, waiting to see what would happen next. After a few moments of silence, the one-eyed creature's voice thundered, as if from above. What he said made him seem far less threatening.

> *I am the father of nine sons,*
> *all one-eyed monster boys.*
> *I keep an eye on all my lads,*
> *as they play with their toys.*
> *A three-eyed monster once dropped in*
> *and brought his sons along.*
> *Three bulging eyes were on each guest;*
> *oh, what a blinking throng!*

Together all the monsters
had exactly forty eyes.
How many three-eyed kids were there?
The numbers tell no lies.

Chapter 4

Jayden's Helper

Alex now found himself at the bottom of the page, where a caption read: "Help Jayden answer this question and then turn the page."

"No way am I doing the math!" Alex said to himself. Impatient to continue reading the rest of the adventure, he tried to go on without working out the answer. But the page would not turn. No matter how hard he pulled, the page stayed glued to the next one. In fact, the whole rest of the book was stuck tight. Alex shook the book, flipped it upside down and even blew on it. Nothing helped.

Disgusted, Alex tossed the book onto his desk. What was this, a bad joke? Some kind of trick thing, like that teeth-blackening "toothpaste" sold at so-called magic shops? Alex laughed. "Some magic!" he said, and then, with dawning excitement, he breathed, "Magic . . . "

Slowly, Alex reached out and picked up the book again. Could it be? He would never have believed it if he hadn't had a magic pencil in his own hands not very long ago. The magic pencil! If he had it right now, Alex would gladly wear it down to a stump to help Jayden. But without the pencil, he could never figure out the first puzzle, let alone four hundred of them. Without the magic pencil, Alex was useless, and Jayden was doomed.

Alex studied the picture of Jayden facing the hideous one-eyed thing. He felt so sorry for the Emerald Queen that he could not bring himself to close the book. What if he tried really hard to solve the puzzle? He had nothing to lose, and the rest of the evening was before him. So Alex took out a pile of paper and an ordinary yellow pencil with an eraser.

Twenty minutes later the floor around his desk was strewn with crumpled sheets. Alex felt as if he had just run a marathon; it was not going well. Gloomily, he stared at the picture. His eye fell on the monster's hands and feet: ten digits on each. Math would be easier with so many fingers and toes to count on . . . forty of them, just like the total number of eyes in the puzzle. Idly, Alex subtracted the fingers that were already occupied holding the diamond-tipped staff. 40 minus 10: the numbers flashed like neon in his mind, and he suddenly knew where to start. On a fresh piece of paper he wrote:

There are 40 eyes in all. To find out how many eyes belong to the guests, the eyes of the one-eyed host family must be subtracted from 40. There is 1 one-eyed father and 9 one-eyed sons, which make 10 eyes. So 40 − 10 = 30 eyes. The guests have 30 eyes altogether. If each one has 3 eyes, 30 must be divided by 3. That makes 10 guests. One of them is the three-eyed father: 10 − 1 = 9. There are 9 three-eyed kids.

After writing down his solution, Alex tried turning the page again. It worked! He saw a picture of Jayden giving a piece of paper to the one-eyed guard. The door behind the monster was opening. Alex was absolutely thrilled. He had done it, and all by himself!

Then he looked closely at the paper in Jayden's hand again and noticed something that made his hair almost stand on end. Not only did her sheet have the same answer as his, but it actually looked like an exact copy of Alex's solution: the same words, the same handwriting, the same layout. Even a smudge that was in the upper right-hand corner of Alex's page appeared in the same place on Jayden's paper.

Incredible! Alex looked around his bedroom, as if trying to find some clue to these unbelievable events. But all he saw was his bed, his closet and his bookshelf. There was not a hint of magic anywhere. Alex was alone, facing the next page of a mysterious, author-less book which was somehow linked to his own world!

Whatever the explanation for all this, Alex was sure of one thing: he had to do everything in his power to prevent Rechner from forcing Jayden into marriage. After reading about the Emerald Queen's bright castle and all that she had left behind, he could not imagine Jayden living in Rechner's dark world for the rest of her life. While he was pondering all this, there was a knock on his door, and he heard his mother's voice: "Lights out soon. Don't forget to brush your teeth."

The next day at school Alex tried to talk to Sam. He wanted to say how truly sorry he was about everything. But most of all Alex wanted to tell him about the book. He was sure Sam would forgive him as soon as he learned about *Jayden's Rescue*. But Sam still seemed to be avoiding Alex and quickly walked away from him the one time they met, by the water fountain.

Fortunately, there was still Vanessa. At lunchtime Alex sought out his understanding friend. Vanessa listened eagerly as Alex described all that he had read and done.

"So why didn't the Idyllian soldiers put on firefighters' gear and rush through the flames?" she wondered with excitement. "Or maybe they could have used a catapult to throw each other over the fire . . . "

"Who knows?" answered Alex. "But that's not the point. The point is that I am part of it, and you can be too. Together we have a far better chance of solving all those puzzles."

"You mean it? Can I come over tonight?"

The two quickly made plans. That evening, when the dessert dishes had been cleared away, Alex flew to his room. Soon after he had finished his homework, the doorbell rang. Vanessa and Alex exchanged secretive glances as they ran up the stairs and headed straight for Alex's bookshelf. When Vanessa saw the book's cover, she exclaimed:

"I can't believe it! You never told me that this silver castle was just like the one on the tip of your pencil!"

Alex looked. "That's why it looked to so familiar last night!" he replied.

Alex waited as Vanessa read all about Jayden's life in Idyllia and her kidnapping by Rechner. Then he showed her his own solution to the first puzzle and the identical solution in Jayden's hand.

"Amazing . . . " Vanessa kept muttering as more and more wondrous things appeared before her.

Now it was time to head straight into the second room of Rechner's dungeon. Jayden's path was blocked by a guard who looked like a bear on bird's legs. One leg was lifted into the air, the way a flamingo stands. Around its neck the creature wore a heavy gold chain with a medallion. His puzzle went like this:

I eat berries soft and juicy — they're my favourite chow.
Keep in mind: five hundred kilos is my weight right now.
I've just finished having supper. What a berry feast!
But I think I overdid it — I'm a greedy beast.
Right before the meal I was a slimmer, lighter bear:
Just four hundred fifty kilos. This is true, I swear!
Each delicious berry weighs ten grams — no more, no less.
Count the berries I have eaten. Be precise; don't guess.

"Why don't you start, Ness," said Alex, handing her a pencil.

"Let's see now." Vanessa looked at the puzzle again. "The beast weighed 450 kilograms before supper and 500 afterwards. That means he must have eaten 50 kilograms' worth of berries. But the berries' weight is given in grams. We need to know how many grams there are in a kilo."

"Where do we find that?" asked Alex, looking worried.

Vanessa reached into her school bag, took out a little plastic card and put it on the desk. "This is a table of weights and measures, the handiest thing in the world," she explained. "You can look up how many centimetres there are in a metre, how many grams in a kilogram and other stuff. My mom gave this to me, and I always keep it in my bag."

"Cool," said Alex, examining the card. "Let's see. A kilo is, um, 1,000 grams. 50 times 1,000 is . . . " He frowned. " . . . 50,000?"

"Yes!" said Vanessa, nodding. "And now we need to know how many berries make up 50,000 grams. Each berry weighs 10 grams, so we just divide 50,000 grams by 10, and get 5,000."

"The glutton ate 5,000 berries!" exclaimed Alex. "No wonder he says he overdid it." He reached out to turn the page.

"Wait!" said Vanessa. "I want to try something." She drew a stick person just underneath their solution and then turned the page in the book. "Wow!" she cried out.

The paper that Jayden was handing to the bird-bear creature had the same stick person under the solution. Alex and Vanessa looked at each other and did not say a word for moment. Then they giggled, exchanged high-fives, and went back into Rechner's castle. They did not stop until it was time for Vanessa to go home.

Every night for the rest of that week, they went from one room to the next. The excitement mounted, but Vanessa and Alex couldn't help worrying. Jayden's freedom depended on them, and it seemed a lot of responsibility for two kids.

"Maybe we should tell your mom and dad or Ms Lund," suggested Vanessa without much conviction.

"Just imagine this conversation, Ness: 'Mom, Dad, I have this book with pages that won't turn unless I solve the puzzle inside . . . ' I know just what they'd say: 'Another wizard story from the library, Al? Sounds interesting. Have you finished your homework?'"

"Or, if I did get them to look at the book, they'd never let me keep it," continued Alex. "They'd have guys in lab coats cutting up the book in some building far away. That would be the end of it for us."

It was now Sunday, the night before Alex's second math test without his magic pencil. Last week's had been a disaster, and Alex's parents were as surprised as Ms Lund. But it was decided that anyone could have a bad day. The Camp Waconda deal was still on, as long as he did better on the next test. So, just before Vanessa came over, Alex went over his math notes from class. Things made a little more sense than they used to. But Alex was still very nervous.

"Hi, Al," said Vanessa, walking into his room and looking as perky as ever. "Are you ready?"

"Sure. Let's get going," replied Alex and opened the book. On the page before them Jayden's way was blocked by a monster who had five heads. Each head had a different expression on its face. One was frowning; another seemed surprised; a third one was smiling; the fourth head looked sleepy; and the fifth was very serious as it spoke:

> *My heads have lots of hair to comb;*
> *it's hard to find the time.*
> *So when I comb a head of hair,*
> *my parents pay a dime.*
> *Each head is combed in sequence,*
> *always one, two, three, four, five.*
> *My mom says order is a goal*
> *for which good monsters strive.*
> *I'm proud to say that now I've earned*
> *twelve dollars fair and square.*
> *How often, tell me, have I combed*
> *each shaggy head of hair?*

"How many dimes are there in twelve dollars?" wondered Vanessa.

"There are 10 dimes in a dollar. 10 times 12 is 120," answered Alex, without even thinking about it. Money math was something he knew about!

"Now let's divide the total by the number of heads the guard has," said Vanessa. She scribbled a bit, and then said, "120 divided by 5 is 24."

"So each head has been combed twenty-four times," said Alex. "This is a cinch!"

Now the test tomorrow seemed a little less scary. They turned the page, and, as always, Jayden's answer looked just like Vanessa's and Alex's. They kept going until they had solved puzzle number 50.

"Alex, I think you'll do fine on the test tomorrow," Vanessa assured her friend as she went out Alex's front door.

Alex just shrugged and waved goodbye. His mind was on Jayden and her progress, not on Monday math. Before getting ready for bed, Alex went over to the desk. The book was still open exactly where they had stopped a few minutes earlier. He was about to shut it and put it back on the shelf when suddenly something strange caught his eye. On the wall of the room where Jayden was now standing there was an inscription. It looked as if it were chiseled right into the stone. Alex was sure that this writing had not been there the last time he looked. Something fishy was going on!

Meddling rescuers, beware!
Keep on puzzling, if you dare.
Aren't you noble! Aren't you bold!
Your heroics leave me cold.
Here's my warning: Jayden's mine.
That is Rechner's bottom line.

R.

So things were not as good as they seemed. The king knew that Alex and Vanessa were helping Jayden, but still, he seemed sure that Jayden would not be able to work her way out of the dungeon.

Alex read the inscription again. He had the feeling that there was another, more threatening message lurking between the lines. What if Rechner did something to Jayden? Or him and Vanessa?

Alex put the book down, telling himself not to be ridiculous. Rechner was a character in a book, and he and Vanessa were safe in the real world. If there was anyone in danger here, it was Jayden. One thing was clear: Jayden had to keep moving, no matter what. They would have to work faster.

Just before he fell asleep, Alex thought of Sam. Perhaps it was time to bring in a third rescuer . . .

Chapter 5

The Message

On the bus the next morning, Alex started talking the moment he sat down next to Vanessa. When he had finished telling her about the threat on the wall of the last room, she shook her head.

"I knew things were going too well," she said. "What do you think he's going to do?"

"I have no idea, but we have to be ready for anything."

"You know, I'd feel a lot better if Sam were on the team," sighed Vanessa. "We could really use someone else. And Sam's pretty smart."

"That's exactly what I was thinking last night!" exclaimed Alex. "But Sam seems kind of mad at me."

"Do you want me to talk to him?" asked Vanessa.

"No, Ness. This is between Sam and me. I'll talk to him later today."

Thinking about Jayden, Rechner and Sam, Alex had forgotten about the Monday morning ordeal. As soon as he walked into the classroom and saw the test papers laid out on each desk, he groaned. He was not sure which was worse, Rechner or Ms Lund's math test. When everyone was settled, Ms Lund told them to begin. Alex looked at the first question and gasped. Then he looked around. Ms Lund was feeding the fish in the aquarium across the room, and all the other kids were busily working away, just like on any Monday morning.

Alex closed his eyes and rubbed them. He took several deep breaths, trying to empty his mind of everything connected with *Jayden's Rescue*. But when he looked again, the first question still read:

Your heart is brave. Your mind is strong.
And Jayden's in your debt.
The quest to free her must go on
despite King Rechner's threat.
If she has covered fifty rooms
and has so many more,
How many will she cross each day
before the final door?
A daily quota must be met,
as steady as the clock.
Five weeks is all that Jayden has
to break the castle lock.

Monoculus

Even after all the incredible events of the previous few weeks, Alex could still hardly believe what he was seeing. Unusual math problems were Ms Lund's specialty. They frequently made even Alex smile. But this was a personal message to him! Who was Monoculus, and how did he know about Rechner's threat?

Alex forgot he was supposed to be afraid of this test. There was no time for that. Jayden had to be out of her prison in five weeks, and it was now crucial to find out how many rooms they needed to cross each day to make the deadline. Slowly, he went over every word of the problem, and the solution began to crystallize in his mind.

There are 400 rooms in Rechner's dungeon. 50 rooms have been crossed, so 350 remain. We have 5 weeks to cross them. There are 7 days in a week: 5 times 7 is 35. We have 35 days to cross the remaining rooms. 350 divided by 35 is 10.

Alex stopped. The answer was ten rooms per day. There was nothing to it. But why five weeks? He and Vanessa would have to figure it out later. Right now the rest of the test was waiting.

Still buoyed by the exhilaration of solving Monoculus's puzzle, Alex eagerly went on to the rest of the questions. They were definitely Ms Lund's – kind of funny, but completely normal. Alex finished in good time. As he was handing in his paper, he whispered to the kid in front of him, "John, what did you get for the first question?"

"Ten," his classmate whispered back.

"Ten what?" asked Alex. Ms Lund was frowning at him, but he had to know.

John gave him a funny look. "Ten push-ups, of course," he answered.

So Alex's first question *was* custom-made. What would happen when Ms Lund marked his test?

At lunchtime Alex hurriedly told Vanessa about the test question. "It was signed 'Monoculus,'" he concluded. "Does the name mean anything to you?"

"I'd remember a name like that if I'd ever heard it."

"So would I. But whoever it is, we now know that there is someone else on Jayden's side. And that someone knows what we are doing. That's good . . . I guess."

"Of course it is, Al," said Vanessa, sounding quite sure of herself. "I wonder how this Monoculus pulled that test question off. And why does Jayden have to get out of the castle in exactly five weeks?"

"That's what I've been wondering," said Alex, unwrapping his sandwich. All around the lunchroom there were kids eating, laughing and acting perfectly normal. To them, nothing incredible was going on; there was no prisoner in an enormous dungeon, no dangerous sorcerer, no monster guardians, no secret messages in test questions. If they only knew what was at stake!

Then Alex and Vanessa heard Sam's voice: "Hey, do either of you have salami? I'm looking to trade."

"I do," said Vanessa, and pulled out a chair. Alex grinned at him, feeling enormous relief. But he felt too embarrassed to say anything.

He didn't have to. Sam broke the ice.

"Guess what!" he said. "I'm going to camp this summer."

"Which one?" asked Vanessa.

"Waconda. My cousin went there last year, and she had a ball."

"Hey, I'm going to the same camp!" replied Vanessa. "That's so cool!"

"So am I!" exclaimed Alex. "As long as I keep my math grades up, that is. That's why I . . . " He trailed off. He didn't want to wreck the moment by mentioning the pencil.

"Do either of you know how to sail?" asked Sam. "I hear you get to do that at Waconda. I can't wait."

He was acting as if nothing had happened. All the time Sam was talking about overnight trips and campfires, Alex kept wondering if his friend had forgotten about the magic pencil.

Then it was time for the most important thing: to tell Sam about Jayden and the magic book. Alex and Vanessa kept interrupting each other in their excitement as they described a few of the puzzles already solved. Sam especially liked the one about one-eyed and three-eyed monsters at a party. It took until the end of the lunch period to explain how the book worked. They also told him about Rechner's threat. Sam didn't seem the least bit surprised by any of it. Perhaps he hadn't forgotten the magic pencil after all.

"Sam, we really need your help to get Jayden out," concluded Vanessa. "Some of the puzzles are not easy."

"This sounds like a job for me!" was Sam's reply. "I can be there tonight around 6:30. Is that okay?"

Then Alex gulped and gathered all his strength for what he was about to say. "Sam . . . I've got something to get off my chest."

"Go ahead, but don't drop it on my foot," Sam laughed.

"I hid the magic pencil so that it wouldn't get used up so quickly," Alex stammered.

"I suspected as much," said Sam and opened his chocolate bar. "That's why I was so mad. It would have been okay if you'd just told me straight out. I can't stand sneaking around. Want a bite?" he added.

"But that's not all," continued Alex after taking a small chunk of chocolate. "Then I really lost the pencil and I wanted to tell you about it . . . "

"Forget it, Al," said Sam dismissively. "We all do stupid things sometimes. I probably overreacted, anyway."

"Put it there," said Alex, stretching his hand toward Sam. Three hands came together over a lunch table. And that was the end of it.

When the day was over, Sam, Alex and Vanessa sat together in the bus. It felt good to be a threesome again.

"Sam, there's one more thing," said Alex as they pulled out of the parking lot. "We'll have to work really hard tonight and every night for five weeks."

"What do you mean? Why five weeks?" asked Sam.

Alex told Sam about the test that he had written that morning. "Last week Ness and I did fifty rooms. But now, according to this Monoculus guy, we have to pick up the pace to ten rooms a day. That's seventy per week."

"I guess it has to be done before the end of school," said Sam.

Alex and Vanessa looked at each other, and Vanessa smacked her forehead with her palm.

"Now why didn't we think of that?" she exclaimed. "You're a genius, Sam!"

Sam shrugged. "Well, whoever this Monoculus is," he concluded, "he's pretty amazing because he knows how long the school year is and that we're leaving afterwards. Freaky stuff . . . "

That evening at supper Alex proudly showed his parents his latest math test.

"I must thank that Vanessa," said Alex's mother. Alex had told her that the reason Vanessa came over so often was to tutor him.

"Vanessa, eh?" teased Nolan, Alex's older brother. "I guess that's why we haven't seen Sam around here for a while."

"It's nothing like that!" Alex protested. "Sam and I just had a small fight, but we've patched it up. He's friends with Vanessa too – in fact, they're both going to Camp Waconda this summer. Isn't that incredible? Sam can't wait to sail, but I'm more interested in water-skiing . . . "

Soon Nolan was giving Alex all kinds of advice about camp life, and to Alex's relief, when Sam and Vanessa arrived Nolan didn't make any embarrassing comments.

Once in Alex's room, Sam could barely restrain himself.

"Where is it? Show it to me, please!" he demanded as his eyes scoured every corner of the room. When he saw the book and looked inside, he was so thrilled that he kept jumping out of his chair and crying out "Awesome!" "Brilliant!" "Far out!"

"Keep it down," shushed Vanessa. "Do you want everyone to find out about it?"

"I can't help it," whispered Sam. "It's even better than I imagined!"

Now it was time to get serious and start on the next puzzle. They were in room fifty-one, where Jayden had been left the night before. This time there was a rather jolly-looking guard on rabbit's legs. The rest of him was human: dressed in a tailcoat with a carnation in his buttonhole. He gave Jayden the following puzzle:

King Rechner once a castle built. He used his magic powers
And on the castle's mighty walls he put twelve silver towers.
Each one is taller than the last, each one beyond compare.
A lofty problem's built for you, so solve it, if you dare.
The smallest tower's twenty metres; tower two, five more.
The third one's height is thirty-five, and then comes tower four.
It is a huge one: fifty-five. So tell me, if you please:
What is the height of number twelve? The answer is a breeze.

"The answer is not a breeze," sighed Alex. "This is the hardest one so far." Then he turned to the others: "Any ideas?"

"Beats me," said Vanessa. "Let's read it again."

They read it four times, and then suddenly Sam said: "I think I know how we should start. Let's try to figure out the pattern in the differences between each tower from 1 to 4. If we do that, we can keep developing this pattern all the way to tower 12."

"Sam to the rescue," said Vanessa. "OK. The first tower

is 20 metres, the second one is 25, the third one is 35 and the fourth one is 55. The first difference is five, then 10, then 20 – "

"It keeps doubling!" cried Alex. "Tower five will be 40 metres higher than tower four!"

"We'd better make a chart or we'll get mixed up before we get to twelve," said Sam.

They wrote down the following:

Tower 1: 20 metres
Tower 2: 25
Tower 3: 35
Tower 4: 55
Tower 5: 55 + 40 = 95
Tower 6: 40 × 2 = 80   → 95 + 80 = 175
Tower 7: 80 × 2 = 160   → 175 + 160 = 335
Tower 8: 160 × 2 = 320   → 335 + 320 = 655
Tower 9: 320 × 2 = 640   → 655 + 640 = 1,295
Tower 10: 640 × 2 = 1,280   → 1,295 + 1,280 = 2,575
Tower 11: 1,280 × 2 = 2,560   → 2,575 + 2,560 = 5,135
Tower 12: 2,560 × 2 = 5,120   → 5,135 + 5,120
                               = 10,255 metres!

"The twelfth tower is 10,255 metres tall!" exclaimed Alex. "Give me five!"

"Give me ten thousand two hundred and fifty-five," laughed Sam, and slapped Alex's and Vanessa's hands.

But they didn't celebrate for long. They had nine more puzzles to do that night. Jayden was counting on them. It was time to turn the page.

Chapter 6

The Paper Path

In room fifty-eight the three friends saw a terrible thing. There was Jayden, facing a bizarre turtle-headed guard dressed in tennis gear and wearing a top hat. But in Jayden's hands there was no more paper: she had run out! She also had just one very short pencil left. Rechner had said that only written answers opened doors in this dungeon. What was she to do? Jayden looked desperate and even seemed to have tears in her eyes. Had all this work been for nothing? Then the kids noticed that she was also casting a side-long glance . . . at them! They had to think of something.

"What if we put a few sheets of paper right into the book and close it?" proposed Sam.

They did this and waited a few moments. But when they

opened the book again, they found their paper where they had left it. Nothing had changed in the room. Jayden was still empty-handed and looked just as downcast as before.

"Remember the stack of paper in the first room?" said Alex. "If we could just get Jayden to run back there and get more . . . "

"What if we tried flipping the pages?" asked Vanessa.

"Why not?" said Sam. "We have nothing to lose."

The pages were turned back until the children saw the one-eyed monster. They were back in the first room, but this time the picture was different. The creature was not just staring at Jayden with his single eye. He was now pointing toward the stack of paper in the corner of the room and . . . grinning!

"Well, what do you know! The one-eyed thing wants to help her!" exclaimed Vanessa. "He wants her to get through."

"I wonder . . . " said Alex staring at the guard's only eye, but now Sam was flipping the pages forward to room fifty-eight. Jayden was once again standing before the turtle creature, and this time she was beaming.

"It worked!" exclaimed Sam. "Ness, you're a genius!"

Jayden was holding many sheets of paper and five new pencils. The turtle guard looked slightly impatient, as if he were eager to get going. And this is what he had to say:

I've many brothers, young and old. We're all ten years apart.
I'm in the middle of the bunch. Let's see if you are smart.
The youngest brother's age is ten: the only age I'll tell.
The rest is tricky, I'm afraid, so listen very well.

With all our ages added up, we've lived twelve hundred years.
How old am I? Please tell me now, and dry up all your tears.

"This is not getting any easier," sighed Vanessa. "What do you think, Sam?"

"Let's start with what we know," said Sam. He took a fresh piece of paper.

"Okay," said Vanessa. "If they are all ten years apart, and the first one is 10 years old, the second one must be 20, the third one 30 and so on. So I guess we just keep adding by tens until we reach 1,200, the total of their ages."

"By the end, we'll know how many brothers there are, and we'll be able to find the middle one," said Alex.

"That's exactly what I was thinking," said Vanessa.

Sam wrote down $10 + 20 + 30 + 40 + 50 + 60 + 70 \ldots$ "My hand is getting sore," he said. "Let's add them up and see what we've got." He was quiet for a moment, then said, "Only 280 years . . . 920 years to go!"

"I'll go on," said Alex. "The next age is 80 years, so $280 + 80 + 90 + 100 + 110 + 120$. That makes only 780: still short of 1,200 by . . . 420 years."

"Can I take it from there?" asked Vanessa. "After 120 comes 130, then 140 and 150. So $780 + 130 + 140 + 150 = 1,200$. There! The rest is easy. We just have to count how many ages we've added up."

Alex counted each addition, including the initial ten. "Fifteen ages altogether," he said. "Which means fifteen brothers altogether – fourteen plus the guard."

"And the guard's in the middle, he says," said Sam. "So he should have seven brothers on each side, younger and older. So he's number . . . eight!"

"And if the guard is the eighth brother," said Vanessa. "He must be 80 years old! We did it!"

The next day, Ms Lund returned the mysterious (for Alex, anyway) math test. When she gave Alex his, she said: "This is much better than the last one. You had me worried for a while."

Alex looked at the mark: B+. It was certainly not the perfection of the tests written with the magic pencil, but for some reason, he was happier about that B+ than all those A+ tests put together.

Then he looked at the first question. The problem had changed – it was now all about exercising. Alex's answer divided 350 push-ups over five weeks into ten per day, just as John had said. How had Monoculus done it?

When Sam and Vanessa came over that night, they all celebrated Alex's B+ by digging into the box of marzipan bars that Alex's uncle had sent from Germany. When all the candy was gone, they got to work, and things went very well at first. As usual, putting their heads together made for some incredible puzzle solving, and Jayden kept moving from one room to the next.

Then came the last puzzle of their daily quota. Jayden was now in a room where the guard, like most of the other monsters, looked strange but friendly enough. He was a wolf with large scarlet wings and a crocodile tail.

"This one is almost cute," said Vanessa.

"Yeah, but he may bite," joked Sam.

They began to read the puzzle:

Exponentia is a planet
where the swarming burbles play.
Multiplying is what burbles
do with pleasure every day.
If two burbles get together
they begin to multiply
No one can keep up with burbles,
and I don't advise you try.
In just four steps, without the
use of any magic tricks,
Two become sixty-five thousand
and five hundred thirty-six.
Luckily for Exponentia,
there are burble-hunting Zites.
Thanks to them the burble numbers
never reach such dizzy heights.
Otherwise the planet's surface
would be quickly overrun.
In a giant sea of burbles,
you would never have much fun!
Tell me how the burbles do it.
What's the pattern to their sport?
Here's a hint for your solution:
it's a fairly squarish sort.

The children stared at each other, back at the puzzle, and then into space.

"First there are 2 burbles and then 65,536?!" said Alex finally.

Sam groaned. "I don't have a clue."

"Neither do I," sighed Vanessa.

They fell silent, all staring at the book. The clock ticked . . . and ticked and ticked . . .

"What do we do now?" said Alex, as if waking from a daze.

"Well, if we can't figure this one out tonight," said Vanessa, "we can always sleep on it and try again tomorrow."

"And what if tomorrow we're still stuck?" asked Sam. "Remember what Monoculus said: ten rooms a day. We have to keep up the pace or we won't finish before the school year is over. And if we can't solve it at all . . . you know what will happen to Jayden."

It was time to call it a night. Sad and frustrated, they said goodbye, and Alex was left alone in his room. Could this really be happening? They had done so well until now. Surely they could figure out the way to move on!

Alex got into bed, then tossed and turned for ages. Finally he fell asleep, only to wake up in complete darkness. He looked at the clock. It was 3 AM! That was very strange: Alex normally never opened his eyes until he heard the heartless alarm clock at seven o'clock. He did not even know what the middle of the night looked like. But now here he was: wide awake and with four hours of time on his hands.

He got out of bed and turned on his desk lamp. *Jayden's Rescue* was still open at the page with the last puzzle. Alex reread every word very slowly, but it made no more sense than before. Then he had an idea: perhaps the one-eyed guard from the first room who had helped Jayden get more paper would help again.

So Alex went back to that page and immediately a

bright smile spread across his face. The one-eyed monster was now holding a fishing net instead of his diamond-tipped staff, and his puzzle had changed:

Ragged Danny was a fisher;
he was poor, his boat was old.
All his life he dreamed of riches;
every day he thought of gold.
He had heard that if a mermaid
ever landed in a net,
She would pay a handsome ransom
and depart with no regret.

In his boat, one frosty morning,
Danny sat, alone and glum.
Deep in thought, he watched the water,
keeping warm with sailor's rum.
Suddenly, he felt a tugging,
and his net began to dance.
Up he pulled. His heart was jumping.
Maybe this was Danny's chance!

First he glimpsed a tail, all scaly.
Was it just another fish?
But a second later Danny knew
— hurray! — he had his wish.
In the boat there was a mermaid.
She was angry as can be.
Danny said to her, "I've got you.
Give me gold, and you'll swim free."

"I will grant your wish, good fisher,"
said the mermaid with a smile.
"Three gold coins is what I give you:
these should make it worth your while.
If you want more money, Danny,
all you have to say is 'Square!'
Pretty soon you won't be fishing —
you will be a millionaire."

Danny took the coins and freed her.
He was feeling mighty fine.
As she dove into the water,
"Square!" he cried — the coins were nine.
Nine gold coins would buy him plenty,
and the fun had just begun.
"Square!" he shouted and was holding
nine times nine . . . Gulp! Eighty-one!
Eighty-one is quite a number,
but it had to be outdone.
"Square!" he said and saw six thousand
and five hundred sixty-one.
What he failed to notice, sadly,
was the water in the boat.
Danny's barque was barely holding.
Would it sink or stay afloat?

Greedy Danny was too eager
to keep going on and on.
"Square!" he gasped and in a second
he, his boat and gold were gone.

Now, you see why mermaid-fishing
may be nasty for one's health?
(Do you know the heavy number
that sank all of Danny's wealth?)

By the time he had reached the end of the story, numbers swirled through Alex's mind like a tornado. What magic had the word "Square!" performed? Alex read the puzzle a second time, and he had the answer: it had multiplied each number by itself! First three coins, then three times three: nine. Then nine times nine: 81. He grabbed his calculator – he didn't have time to try it out on paper. Sure enough, 81 times 81 equalled 6,561. That's how many coins Danny had just before his boat sank. Fingers trembling, Alex punched in 6,561 times 6,561. The answer was 43,046,721! No wonder the boat went down. So many coins would have sunk even a trawler.

Alex jumped up to phone Sam and Vanessa. Then he remembered what time it was and sat down at his desk again. Almost tearing the pages of the book in his haste, Alex leafed forward until he was back in the room with the wolf-crocodile guard. He grabbed some paper and wrote,

2×2 burbles $= 4$

"Square!" he whispered to himself, and smiled. He went on, moving so quickly he nearly broke his pencil.

$4 \times 4 = 16$
$16 \times 16 = 256$

$256 \times 256 = 65,536$

There it was: 65,536 burbles in just 4 steps. It was so beautifully simple!

Nothing seemed impossible now. Alex tried to turn the page, and it turned. Jayden's solution was, as always, identical to his. Now Jayden could go into the next room. A blue unicorn with eight legs awaited her.

Alex yawned and crawled back into bed. As he began to doze off, he was suddenly jolted by the frightening thought that the "square" puzzle's solution had been a dream. He got out of bed again to check. Brilliant! Jayden was indeed standing beside the eight-legged unicorn, waiting for her rescuers.

Chapter 7

Surprise

"What are you so happy about, Al?" Sam asked the next morning on the bus. He looked like he hadn't slept all night. "I've been thinking about those silly multiplying burbles non-stop, and I still have no solution."

"But Jayden does," laughed Alex, unable to keep it to himself any longer, "and she's in the next room already. You'll really like the unicorn."

"What unicorn? What are you talking about?" exclaimed Vanessa.

Alex took out the book.

"Hey, why did you bring that here?" whispered Sam and looked around the bus. "What if something happens to it?!"

"Don't worry, I'll be really careful." Alex opened the book and watched with pleasure as Sam and Vanessa looked at the solution in Jayden's hand, at the unicorn monster and then at Alex.

"How did you do it? You're a brain if there ever was one, Al!" said Sam.

Vanessa went over the numbers. "It works. This 'square' stuff is so cool!"

"I had help," confessed Alex. "Let me show you." And he turned to the one-eyed monster's page. The sad story about Danny and the mermaid was still there.

"I bet this one-eyed guard knows everything that's going on," said Vanessa. "I guess the rescue team has a fourth member. If we get into trouble again, we'll know where to turn."

The end of the school year drew closer and closer, but Alex, Vanessa and Sam were old pros, now, and solved ten puzzles a day without fail. Occasionally they were a little stumped, but their one-eyed friend was always ready to assist them. They became very fond of him and sometimes even visited his page just to say hello.

However, Alex still wondered about Rechner's threat. Surely the sorcerer had not been bluffing. As Jayden moved closer and closer to the exit, Alex's feeling that things were going far too smoothly grew stronger and stronger.

In the last week of school, Ms Lund introduced a new topic in math. She wrote 5^2 on the board and said: "Does anyone know what 5 squared is?"

Alex looked around. No one's hand was raised, not even Laura Chi's. Should he do it? Why not?! Slowly, Alex put up his hand.

"Yes, Alex?" said Ms Lund.

"I think 5 squared is . . . 25?"

"Exactly!" Ms Lund wrote the answer on the board: $5^2 = 25$. "Have you been doing some extra math on your own, Alex?"

He blushed and muttered: "Kind of . . . "

Then Ms Lund explained that the little number to the right and above the number 5 was called an exponent. The exponent ^{2} meant that the number had to be multiplied by itself once: $5^2 = 5 \times 5$. The exponent ^{3} meant one more multiplication: $5^3 = 5 \times 5 \times 5$. And so on.

Exponent! The planet of the burbles was called Exponentia! Alex couldn't help grinning.

After the bell, as Alex was about to leave for recess, Ms Lund stopped him and asked, "I suppose you are using some kind of math workbook, Alex. I'm curious to know what it is."

Alex was suddenly aware of the weight of *Jayden's Rescue* in his backpack. He felt his face get hot as he stared at his teacher. Then, barely able to control his voice, he said: "It's a book of . . . math puzzles."

"Sounds neat! Do you have it with you? I'd love to see it. There are other students in the class who would benefit from the kind of work you've been doing."

Alex didn't know what to do. Fortunately, at that moment another teacher stopped outside the door and called to Ms Lund. Alex made his escape.

On the night before the last day of school, Alex was still eating supper when Sam and Vanessa arrived at the door.

"Would you like some dessert?" Alex's mother asked them, but Alex said, "No time, Mom. We have a lot of . . . homework to do. We'd better get started."

His family stared.

"What homework?" said Nolan suspiciously. "Teachers don't give homework the night before the last day of school. What are you guys up to?"

"We're planning what we're going to do at Camp Waconda," Vanessa said swiftly.

"Well, it's your turn to load the dishwasher," Alex's mother reminded him.

"We'll help," offered Sam. "C'mon, Alex."

"Good one, Vanessa," Alex said quietly, as the three scraped and rinsed with a clatter. "Once Nolan smells a rat, he doesn't let go until it's caught. But I think you got him off the scent."

The first nine puzzles went off without any trouble. However, when they reached room four hundred, the very last one, they gasped. Jayden stood before a locked door, and no monster guard was around to offer a way through. She was stuck.

"I bet Rechner was never going to give her a chance," said Alex bitterly. "This door was probably not meant to be opened by Jayden, no matter what."

"What a skunk!" fumed Vanessa. For the first time the boys saw something resembling a look of anger on her face.

Sam peered at the picture until his nose was almost touching the page. "Aha!" he cried.

He pointed to the locked door. Over the doorknob there was a dial with numbers from one to sixty, just like the combination locks on school lockers.

"Where there's a combination lock, there's a combination," said Sam.

"What are we supposed to do – try out every combination of three numbers from 1 to 60 until we hit on the right one?" asked Vanessa with disgust. "That would take way too long. Unless we managed to slip Jayden a computer and program!"

"And anyway," said Sam, "even if we did crack the code, who would we give the solution to? There's no monster here."

"There's always the one-eyed monster," suggested Alex.

So they returned once again to the first room. However, what they saw did not make them happy at all. Their favourite guard was not there.

"He's left us just when we need him most!" groaned Vanessa, but Alex calmly flipped the pages again. Vanessa heaved a sigh of relief. Back in room 400, Jayden was no longer alone. The one-eyed monster guard stood in front of her. And Jayden looked as relieved as the kids.

"I knew we could count on him," said Alex.

" 'Count' is the word," said Sam.

This is what the creature had to say to Jayden:

Old Rechner is the meanest king that I have ever seen.
I've learned he's played a trick on you, so you would be his queen.
He put no monster at this door, and you will find no key.
But such a tyrant I won't serve. I want to set you free.

King Rechner has a secret chest that's full of wondrous things:
A cloak that helps him move unseen, and wands, and magic rings.
But of them all, he treasures most a pencil made for math.
Its job is clearing all that blocks a problem-solver's path.

Black magic needs astrology. You can't get very far
Unless you deftly calculate the movements of each star.
Whenever Rechner casts a spell that's meant to hurt or maim,
The pencil figures faultlessly and sharpens Rechner's aim.

Before he brought you here to us, King Rechner went away.
He often prowls through far-off lands, but where, I cannot say.
On his return, the castle rang with Rechner's angry cries,
For on his travels he had dropped his number-crunching prize.

A few weeks later he was gone again, but not for long.
"I've got it back! It's mine once more!" was Rechner's merry song.
And with that pencil he designed a trial you're doomed to fail,
So that, despairing, you will wed the king to leave his jail.

Rechner's chest is known to none — but I'm a clever spy
And nothing ever hides from me and my all-seeing eye.
So when I heard King Rechner boast that he had tricked his "guest,"
I was resolved to help you leave, and broke into his chest.

So many puzzles you have solved. One more is left to do.
Monoculus has done his job. The rest is up to you.

The kids saw the guard handing Jayden a silver pencil with little blue numbers all over it. There was no eraser on the end, but rather, a miniature castle . . .

Alex jumped straight up into the air, upsetting all the papers on his desk. He was so agitated that at first only his lips moved: no sound came out of his mouth at all. And then, like water breaking through a dam, his elated voice reverberated throughout the room:

"There it is! The magic pencil! Now I know where it came from. It was Rechner's pencil that I found at the bus stop. It was his footsteps that I heard that morning. He must have dropped the pencil as he walked past me in his invisibility cloak. And then he stole it back out of my locker."

After the meaning of this amazing discovery had sunk in, the kids caught their breath and for a moment no one said a word.

"So the whole puzzle thing was just a ploy," Sam broke the silence. "It was supposed to wear Jayden out so much that the last door would break her!"

"Hey, look at the monster's name!" cried Vanessa.

The boys went back to the one-eyed creature's words and immediately Alex was out of his chair again. "Monoculus!" he shouted. "The test question! What a monster! What a pal!"

"Well, that's one puzzle solved," said Sam. "But we still don't have the puzzle for room 400. So how on earth can we help Jayden to open this door?"

After another moment of silence, Vanessa said, "One thing is clear: Monoculus has done all he could. So there's no point in going back to his room again."

Alex replied: "But there's no point in going forward either. After the last room there's nothing left except the back cover . . . "

He stopped. Sam's and Vanessa's jaws dropped when they saw what Alex had stumbled upon. In the middle of the back cover there was a little door: not a picture, but a real door with tiny hinges and a little silver knob. Beside the knob was the same dial that the children had just seen on the other side, with numbers from one to sixty. Alex nudged it with his fingertip. It turned.

"This is totally weird," said Alex. "I don't remember seeing this door here before. And I've looked at the back cover many times."

Then, they noticed some very faint writing inscribed in circles all around the dial:

To open me you need to know two numbers: X and Y.
There is a third one: 42. Now let me clarify:
When X and Y are added up they're half of 42.
And Y is twice as big as X. I'll say no more to you.

M.

"X! Y! Those aren't numbers!" said Sam.

"This puzzle is way beyond us," said Vanessa.

"Monoculus may as well not have put any puzzle here at all," sighed Alex. "How can we solve this? Nolan does math like that – I think it's called algebra."

"Ah, but Monoculus gave Jayden the pencil," reminded Vanessa.

"That? It's just a picture on the last page," said Sam.

"Is it, now?" smiled Vanessa and opened the book at room 400. Tucked into the binding was the pencil, not a picture any more, but real. It was shorter than when Alex had last seen it, and the point was worn.

Alex handed the pencil to Sam. "Here, I meant to give this to you a long time ago."

"Thanks," said Sam and touched a piece of paper with the pencil. Of course, the pencil began to write:

$$(X + Y) \times 2 = 42$$
$$42 \div 2 = 21$$
$$X + Y = 21$$
$$X \times 2 = Y$$
$$X + (X \times 2) = 21$$

Then it stopped. Sam lifted the pencil and looked at the nearly flat lead. "It really needs sharpening."

"Sam, be careful," warned Alex as Sam put the pencil in the electric sharpener on the desk. "Don't push too hard."

"Don't worry," replied Sam. "It's not as if I've never sharpened a pencil before." He pushed the pencil into the sharpener and . . .

"Help!" Sam shrieked, frantically trying to pull the pencil out. "It's stuck!" The sharpener was greedily eating up their last centimetres of hope. Even though Alex lunged to save the pencil, it was too late. There was nothing left but the castle-tower tip.

"I'm really sorry," said Sam, looking completely devastated. Alex felt equally shattered as he held the remains of the pencil.

But Vanessa was her usual optimistic self. "Look at it this way: the pencil has probably done the hardest part of the puzzle. Why don't we try to do the rest ourselves?"

"Sure, why not?" sighed Sam. "The worst that can happen is that we'll fail."

Alex carefully put the little castle tower down and

looked over the partial solution. "Aside from the Xs and Ys, everything but the brackets looks normal. Does anyone know what the brackets mean?"

Sam and Vanessa shook their heads.

"Why don't you ask your brother?" asked Sam.

"No way! He'll want to know why I'm asking, and before you know it he'll be in here trying to find out!" said Alex emphatically. He turned to Vanessa. "But you could ask. For some reason, he always acts polite around you."

Vanessa blushed, which Sam and Alex both thought very interesting. But she went, coming back a little later looking triumphant.

"Brackets mean you do those parts first," she said. "And the letters stand for numbers you don't know. The point of algebra seems to be that you fiddle around with the numbers you know, arranging them in different equations with the letters and stuff, until you're able to figure out what the value of the letters should be."

Sam and Alex stared at their friend with admiration.

"All right, Ness," said Sam.

Vanessa grinned. "Back to work," she said.

"Let's take the last part, $X + (X \times 2) = 21$, and plug in some numbers for X. We'll just pick anything to start with," said Alex.

"How about 5?" said Sam and began to write. "5 times 2 is 10, 5 plus 10 is 15. Nope, 5 doesn't work. It's supposed to equal 21."

"Let's try 6 then," proposed Vanessa. "6 times 2 is 12, plus 6 is 18. Still not quite 21. Maybe 7?"

Alex wrote, $7 + (7 \times 2) = 21$. "That's it!"

"So X = 7," said Sam. "And Y is supposed to be twice 7, so it must be 14. X is 7; Y is 14. Together they make 21 and 21 x 2 makes the known number: 42. So 7 and 14 fit all the equations."

"And they must be the first and second numbers of the combination," concluded Alex. "The third one is 42, according to the puzzle."

Alex took a deep breath and began to turn the dial on the back cover. A couple quick turns to the left, then he settled on 7. A full turn to the right, past 7, and on until he stopped at 14. Then a turn to the left until he was at 42. A quick tug, and —

"It's not working!" cried Alex.

The rescue team was cast into despair — but only for a moment. There are only six possible ways of combining three numbers, and it took just a couple of minutes to figure out the right one: 14–42–7. They heard a click, and the door was no longer locked.

"Well, here it goes." Alex nervously glanced at the others and tugged on the knob.

At that instant the lights flashed and went out. Immediately they heard Nolan's irritated voice. "Hey, do you mind? I'm studying for a physics final! Who turned out the lights?! Are you up to something, Alex?"

"It must be a power failure," said Alex's father from another room. "I'll go check the fuse box."

A few minutes later the lights went back on. The kids stared at the book. The door was wide open. They rushed to look at the last page; it was empty. Jayden was free.

But where had she gone?

Chapter 8

Camp Waconda

The bus ride to camp was long and tiring. Sam, Vanessa and Alex hardly spoke at all. Too much had happened in their lives, and they needed time to think about everything. The fields and trees along the highway seemed to stretch on eternally, broken up only by an occasional farm or gas station. All around kids were singing, playing cards and making quite a racket.

Alex had packed very carefully the night before. His clothes, beach towel, hat, sunglasses, insect repellent, sunscreen and many other essentials were placed into an old suitcase. The last thing to go in was *Jayden's Rescue*. He had agreed with Sam and Vanessa that it would come with them to camp. After weeks of furious puzzle-solving, they were reluctant to let their adventure end with just an empty room. Where had Jayden gone, through the door they had helped her open? Had she made it back to Idyllia? Or was she somewhere else? They had no idea, but they were all hoping the book would tell them . . . somehow.

Alex's mother caught a glimpse of *Jayden's Rescue* in his suitcase and said, "What an odd-looking book. I've never seen this one before. Where did you get it, Alex?"

This time Alex had enough presence of mind to say, "Well, it's not from the library, if you're worried about a fine, Mom."

He quickly threw a sweatshirt over the book and added, "So what time does the bus leave tomorrow?"

"You know, I forgot to check," replied his mother and rushed out of the room. Alex heaved a sigh of relief and shut the suitcase.

His mother called up from downstairs. "The buses leave at eight-thirty, and we're supposed to be at the parking lot at eight o'clock. You'd better go to bed early tonight."

When Alex's father tucked him in he said, "Isn't it great that Sam and Vanessa are going too? You'll have friends right away. I remember being kind of lonely at first when I went to camp."

Alex *did* feel a bit worried. This was his first trip away from home without his family. He thought he was old enough to handle it, but you never know what might come up. At the same time, he could not wait until morning.

At seven-thirty, after a pancake breakfast and a final check of his luggage, Alex and his family left the house.

When they arrived in the parking lot full of buses, Alex hugged his mom and dad, promised to phone as soon as he got there, and climbed into bus number seven. It was very different from his school bus. This bus had plush, comfortable seats, big tinted windows, elbow rests, air conditioning, a washroom in the back and even TVs. What a treat! Alex quickly spotted Sam and Vanessa who were already sitting together.

"Hi, guys," said Alex and settled into the seat across the aisle.

"Did you remember to bring it?" whispered Sam.

"It's in my suitcase. My mom noticed it last night and started asking questions, but I talked my way out of it."

"I'm still really bothered by one thing," said Vanessa as the bus started moving. "Rechner's threat. How come it never amounted to anything?"

"Why worry?" put in Sam. "It just means Rechner was bluffing. He probably couldn't do anything anyway."

"I'm not so sure," said Vanessa. "He's been in our world before. He'll come back sooner or later."

When they arrived at Camp Waconda, it was already late afternoon. The first thing that Alex felt upon getting off the bus was . . . a mosquito bite. Good thing he had brought his spray.

Everyone ran toward a man in a beige fishing hat. He had a thick mustache and a permanent smile on his face that made him look like a happy cat. On his T-shirt it said Camp Director Jeff.

"Welcome to Camp Waconda!" he announced through a hand-held loudspeaker. "I am your friendly director. My name is Jeff, but my friends call me . . . Jeff. Ha ha! You must all be very tired after such a long ride. Next time we'll try to move the camp closer to the city."

The kids were too exhausted to laugh, but Jeff seemed at least pretty cool. He sorted the campers into age groups and sent each group to its cabin. Sam and Alex were together, but Vanessa's cabin was on the other side of the camp, in the girls' glen. They agreed to meet at suppertime in the mess hall.

The cabins turned out to be really simple but cozy: ceiling, floor, door, two windows and six bunk beds. Alex climbed up to the top bunk of the first bed he saw. Sam collapsed on the bottom bunk. Summer was finally here.

In a few days Alex, Vanessa and Sam felt like they could stay at Camp Waconda forever. It was better than they could ever have imagined. Sailing turned out to be Sam's passion. Alex and Vanessa did not have to ask where Sam was headed after breakfast every morning: the sailing dock was the only possible place. By the end of the first week Sam could rattle off the name of every part in a sailboat and tie ten different knots, which he never tired of demonstrating to Alex and Vanessa. "It's the America's Cup for you," commented Vanessa, watching Sam duck expertly as the boom swung around.

What Alex and Vanessa liked most was water-skiing. It was much easier than they had expected. They started with a board but could soon get up on twin skis and go around the lake with only one or two wipeouts. By the second week, neither of them fell and they could even ski while holding the tow rope with just one hand. It was especially nice to have a free hand to wave in Sam's direction while zooming past his sailboat. As the days went by, Vanessa's favourite trick became crossing the wake back and forth. As for Alex, he eventually learned to put the rope between his knees and wave to Sam with both hands.

The rest of the time was taken up with such things as arts and crafts, games, hikes, archery and dancing. In the evening there was usually a campfire with never a shortage of fireside songs. The food wasn't bad, although Sam grumbled that there wasn't nearly enough salami. Two times already the kids had gone on overnight canoe trips. They slept in tents, cooked hot dogs over a fire and once even saw a real live moose swimming across the lake in the rays of the setting sun!

Jayden's Rescue was kept safely in Alex's suitcase under the bunk bed. A couple of times Alex looked through the book but didn't notice anything new. Jayden seemed to have vanished without a trace. Oh, well. They had done their job: solved four hundred puzzles and freed the Emerald Queen. There was nothing left to do. Besides, camp kept the rescue team so busy that they eventually stopped thinking about the book altogether.

One morning Alex was awakened by the sound of doves cooing right next to the cabin. He had water-skied all night long in his dreams and was disappointed to find himself in bed rather than in the wake of a supersonic boat, heading off into infinite waters.

Sam was already up and getting dressed. "Quick, let's get to breakfast. They said I could try sailing the catamaran today."

At the mess hall Vanessa was already making herself a second piece of toast. She covered it with peanut butter and brown sugar.

"What took you guys so long?" she asked. "Do you want to miss all that sunshine?"

Sitting down and pouring some milk on his cereal, Sam asked, "So what are you going to do after breakfast, Ness? Wait, don't tell me . . . Will you, by chance, be water-skiing with Alex?"

"However did you guess?!" exclaimed Vanessa with a note of dramatic surprise. "And you, perhaps, will be . . . sailing? How's that for fortune-telling? Well, you can watch us whiz by from your *snailboat.*"

"*Snailboat?*" exclaimed Sam with indignation. "I'll have you know that a sailboat is a work of art. While you dangle at the end of a rope, shaking and struggling to stay up behind a noisy, smelly motor crocodile, I gracefully glide through the waters like a beam of light!"

No one had any doubt that another perfect Waconda day was in the making.

At the ski dock Alex and Vanessa put on their life-jackets and got in line. There were only three other kids ahead of them and no one behind. That meant at least one extra turn! On the far side of the lagoon they could see the sailing dock and Sam busily setting up the sails on the red-and-white catamaran.

When it was Vanessa's turn to ski, she pulled out all the stops. She didn't cross the wake, she soared over it. Back and forth, back and forth, Vanessa wove her way behind the boat, much to the admiration of Ron, the ski instructor. She gave him the thumbs-up signal, and Ron increased the speed of the boat. The waves reached Sam and rocked the catamaran.

Then it was Alex's turn. He checked the fasteners on his life jacket, put on the skis that Vanessa had taken off and jumped into the water. The motor roared, the rope tightened and the familiar tug propelled Alex into his favourite element. But as soon as Alex was up and looking forward to another exhilarating ride, there was a crisp scissor-like sound, and the tow rope snapped! As he sank into the water Alex felt his life jacket slipping off his body and leaving him. He kept going down, down – deep below the surface.

Alex had never felt such icy water before. The skis had come off during the fall, too, so there was nothing helping him to stay afloat. He was normally a pretty good swimmer, but in his shock, he lost track of which way was up and panicked. Darkness was all around him. Then a glimmer of light beckoned to him from above. He frantically waved his arms and legs, clawing his way back up toward the sky. As soon as he came up to the surface of the water, he gasped for air, but in a moment he went down again, with a mouthful of lake. Suddenly he felt a splash above his head, and, as he struggled for air a second time, he bumped into a life buoy.

Pale, nauseous, his teeth chattering, Alex hung onto the orange ring for dear life. Where was Ron and the boat? Time seemed to drag endlessly. Alex felt his legs going numb. His hold around the life buoy tightened even more, and a spasm of sheer terror turned his mind blank.

Just then someone's strong hand grabbed Alex and yanked him out of the water. Ron, who looked as if he himself had almost drowned, was staring at Alex and asking: "Are you OK? Speak to me! Can you breathe? How many fingers am I holding up?"

Alex lay in the middle of the motor boat, coughing up water and crying. The day had not turned out quite as perfect as expected.

Back at the ski dock, Alex was helped out of the boat. Vanessa sat down beside him and put her towel around his shoulders. Soon Sam was there too. He had seen everything from the middle of the lake, docked the catamaran and rushed over as quickly as he could. A couple of minutes later Alex was feeling better. Colour was coming back to his face and he was no longer shivering.

By this time Jeff had arrived, alerted about the accident.

"What happened?" he asked, no longer looking at all like a happy cat. "Are you all right?" Alex nodded.

Ron looked very embarrassed as he stammered through an explanation. "I . . . I . . . I've never seen anything like this. It was a brand new rope! I bought it two weeks ago. I still have the receipt."

Jeff took the rope from Ron and examined it closely: "Hey, this thing was cut! I don't like the looks of this, Ron. Let's suspend water-skiing for now. We have to figure out what's going on here."

Alex, Vanessa and Sam also looked at the rope. There was no doubt about it. The rope had been cleanly sliced in two. How could a taut rope have been cut in the middle of a lake behind a moving boat?

"And what about your life jacket?" said Ron. "Didn't you do it up?"

"I sure did," said Alex. "I even double-checked the buckles."

"Well, as I said, there'll be no more skiing. I'll post a sign at the beach," sighed Jeff and put his hand on Alex's head. "Maybe you should go see the nurse."

"No, really, I feel fine now. Don't worry about me." Alex attempted to smile. Then he turned to Ron and said: "Thanks a lot. You came just in time."

"I deserve only half the thanks," said Ron. "It was Vanessa who threw the life buoy."

Alex turned to Vanessa and gave her a big hug. "Another rescue," he whispered in her ear.

Ron and Jeff walked off, leaving Vanessa, Alex and Sam on the dock.

They were about to go too when they were stopped in their tracks by a sudden hissing sound, as if something were bubbling up from below the planks. They looked into the lake and froze. Staring straight at them from the shimmering depths was Rechner's face, looking as angry as it did in the picture where he proposed marriage to Jayden and was rejected.

Vanessa gasped. "Here it comes. I knew it wasn't over."

No one else was on the ski dock or even close by. Ron had taken the motorboat somewhere. The lifeguard was busy doing something near the sailing dock. Alex, Sam and Vanessa felt as if they were pinned to the spot, unable to tear their gaze away from the hideous image in the lake. Then the face spoke, in a hoarse, metallic-sounding voice that seemed to be coming from nowhere.

A bluff, you say? Does Rechner bluff?
The game is up: you've played enough.
It's time to pay for all you've done.
Don't kid yourselves; you haven't won.
You snatched my pencil and my bride!
And then you thought you'd run and hide?!
Well, think again. I play for keeps.
Whoever steals from Rechner, weeps.
I cut your rope; you couldn't float —
I could have sunk that motorboat.
But I will give you one more chance,
Although I warn you in advance:
If Jayden's not brought back to me
in seven days, I'll take you three.

The reflection began to dissipate until only the clouds and sun remained mirrored in the water. The kids looked at each other in absolute dismay. "She was never his bride!" exclaimed Sam. "What a liar!"

"And we don't have her," said Vanessa thoughtfully, "though Rechner seems to think we do. So I guess she's not in Idyllia or Rechner's kingdom. She must have gone right out of the book!"

"And your point is . . . ?" asked Sam.

"Look, we've got to face facts," said Vanessa in a very sober tone of voice. "If Jayden can get out of Rechner's dungeon through the book, than we can just as easily end up *inside* Rechner's dungeon the same way."

"Yeah," agreed Alex, "after what we've been through, I wouldn't rule it out."

Once again it was agreed that seeking help from adults would be pointless. A sorcerer blackmailing three campers over a queen who's escaped from a magic book somehow wouldn't cut it as an emergency situation.

"Let's go back to our cabin," said Alex, and slowly stood up. His legs felt very rubbery, and he leaned on Sam's shoulder. All three of them cast a final look toward the water where Rechner's image had loomed a few minutes earlier. But not a trace of magic disturbed the calm surface of the lake.

Chapter 9

The Way Out

In times like these a monster's advice is essential. In Sam's and Alex's cabin they pulled *Jayden's Rescue* out of the suitcase and turned to the only place where they thought help might be expected: Monoculus's room. And Monoculus did not disappoint them. He had an urgent message waiting for them on a scroll in his left hand.

Even though you're all in danger,
let me offer you a way
to defy the villain's magic,
stand your ground and win the day.
If a secret word is spoken
right to Rechner's wicked face,
Rechner will be locked forever
in this godforsaken place.
I cannot reveal directly
this amazing countercharm.
If I did, it would be toothless
and could cause no wizard harm.
You must pry it out of puzzles:

there are seven nuts to crack.
Then add up the seven answers
and prepare for your attack.

"So all we have to do is figure out this magic word," said
Vanessa. "And Rechner will end up a prisoner in his own
dungeon."

Sam grumbled, "That's exactly what he deserves, but I
sure wish Monoculus could just tell us the spell and get it
over with."

"But don't you see," said Alex impatiently. "Monoculus
said that the word won't work if it's revealed directly. It's
like a quest – you have to sweat for it. That's how it works
in all the books I've read."

Sam looked unconvinced. "Haven't we just finished a
quest?" he objected. "Four hundred puzzles is a pretty
respectable number."

"Well, we don't have much choice," said Vanessa. "And
we ought to be grateful to Monoculus for his help."

Just then a whole throng of campers rushed into the
cabin. They had all heard about the water-skiing accident,
and now they surrounded Alex, showering him with questions. Did he see a monster? Did a mad diver come up from
below and cut the rope? Did he see his whole life pass
before his eyes? Would he ever water-ski again? Sam quickly put the book away as Alex tried to deal with this unwel-
come barrage.

The rescue team now had a problem of another sort.
Seven puzzles would require a big chunk of time and a nice
quiet spot where they wouldn't be disturbed. Where and

when would they get that? Soon everyone was supposed to head off to lunch. Then there were the afternoon activities. After that came supper and campfire. And nine o'clock was lights-out.

"One thing is clear," said Alex as they walked toward the obstacle course after lunch, "we're not going to get a chance to do the puzzles during the day."

"I have an idea," said Vanessa. "What if we sneak out of our cabins at night?"

"But even if we make it past our own counsellors," said Alex, "there's the night patrol. No matter where we sit down with the book, they'll come across us sooner or later. They're bound to notice our flashlights."

"Not if we're on Blackwell Island!" exclaimed Sam. "I know where the spare key for the boats is kept. I'll borrow it one evening and we can sail around the point to the island. No one will bother us there."

"But Blackwell Island doesn't belong to the camp," objected Alex. "Don't you remember? Jeff said it's private property."

"Yeah, but he also mentioned that no one lives there, so I don't see any problem," said Sam triumphantly.

Alex hesitated for a while but finally agreed. "Okay. Let's go tonight. We'll meet at the waterfront at eleven o'clock."

"No way," said Vanessa. "If you think I'm going to walk through the woods alone . . . "

"You're right," said Alex. "I wouldn't do that either. Sorry. We'll come to pick you up just before eleven. Wait behind the big oak tree next to your cabin. And put some stuff into your sleeping bag so that it will look like some-one's in it. You never know when a counsellor might decide to do a bed check."

At campfire that night Alex, Sam and Vanessa were too anxious to do much singing or marshmallow roasting. They were the first ones in their cabins to get to bed, and still 10:49 PM came too soon. Alex and Sam stuffed some clothes into their sleeping bags and snuck out of their cabin. The woods at that time of night don't feel like the best place for a stroll, especially when you suddenly realize that you've forgotten the most important thing – the book! In their nervous haste they had left it under Sam's pillow. So they had to backtrack as fast as they could. That's when they almost woke up Rick, their counsellor. He stirred, and the boys held their breath. After a moment he was still again. Silently they tiptoed outside, put *Jayden's Rescue*, a notepad and some pens into Alex's knapsack and headed toward the girls' glen. They crept almost on all fours to avoid detection.

As soon as they reached Vanessa's cabin, she stepped out from the shadow of a towering oak tree.

"How did it go, Ness?" asked Alex.

"I don't think I like this very much," replied Vanessa, visibly shaken. "I almost woke my counsellor when I dropped my shoe."

"You should have seen us," said Sam. "Okay, guys, let's take my usual shortcut to the sailing docks. Hopefully the patrols don't use that path very much. It's a pretty steep drop past the basketball courts."

Just then the kids had to make an immediate dash behind the washrooms, for at that very moment a beam of light had streaked across the trees toward them. They had barely hidden behind some bushes before the patrol walked by, only a metre away. Then it was all clear, and they reached the lake five minutes later.

The jagged clouds hung low in the ominous sky, but there was enough moonlight to see the boats clearly. A slight breeze made the water lap underneath the sailing dock, and the boats swayed back and forth like giant swans. The kids would have liked to take the sleek catamaran but decided that its absence would be noticed immediately if the patrol came down to the beach. So they picked out one of the small green boats.

Working like a pro, Sam set up the rigging, attached the sail, jumped in and whispered: "Ready!" Smoothly, silently, Sam steered out of the lagoon, over the open waters of the lake and around the point toward Blackwell Island. Alex and Vanessa could see they were wrong about "snailboats." Under Sam's steady hand, the craft seemed to fly almost as fast as someone on water skis. Sam looked very proud. And why not?

"We could never have snuck away like this in a motorboat," said Vanessa, "even if we did know how to drive one. Way to go, Cap'n!"

Thirty minutes later the three sailors arrived in a cove on the island. The first thing they saw was a big "No Trespassing. No Hunting" sign. His fingers flying, Sam quickly attached the boat to a large log jutting out into the lake. Then he took down the sail. Holding their knapsacks above their heads, Alex, Sam and Vanessa waded to shore. The lonely island was very quiet, but the bugs were out in force. And no one had thought to take any repellent along. It was not going to be a comfortable experience.

After hiking inland for several minutes, they found an open spot with a flat tree stump, a perfect table for the book. Alex and Sam took out paper and pencils.

"What have you got in your bag?" asked Sam, pointing to Vanessa's bulging knapsack.

"You didn't think I'd forget to pick up supplies at the tuck shop, did you?" As she emptied the bag's contents on the forest floor, the boys almost forgot why they had come to Blackwell Island. Three bottles of juice, three bananas, three chocolate bars and a large bag of peanuts were strewn around the stump. A regular feast! Then Alex's flashlight lit up a small flat card, which was clearly not part of their midnight snack.

"That's funny," exclaimed Vanessa, picking up the card. "It's my table of weights and measures. I'm sure I left it at home in my school bag. I distinctly remember thinking that I'd never need something like this in summer camp."

The three exchanged looks. "Who knows how it got into your knapsack," said Sam, "but I have the feeling this is no fluke."

Now they were ready to open the book. There was Monoculus, as expected; and this time, instead of his previous message about the magic word, Monoculus's first puzzle was waiting.

Five hungry fish swam out one day
to see what they could eat:
They thought they'd catch a shrimp or two:

that would have been a treat.
Arranged in sequence by their weight,
each one weighed thrice as much
as the one before it in the line —
such order in the clutch!
The peckish second-smallest fish
decided not to wait
And swallowed up the smallest one
as if it were some bait.
The middle fish was keen to feed,
and in voracious haste
It feasted on the second one,
which had a tangy taste.
The second-biggest was no fool
and did not waste its time.
The middle fish was gobbled up;
its flavour was sublime.
The party had to end because
the biggest feaster came
And ate the second-biggest one
without the slightest shame.
That glutton's weight in kilograms
is what I want from you
If just before the meal he weighed
one hundred sixty-two.

As the kids pored over Monoculus's words, they felt as if the old puzzle-solving days had never ended. Only now, instead of the familiar cozy atmosphere of Alex's bedroom, they were surrounded by darkness, rustling leaves and billions of very hungry mosquitoes.

"Wait a second," exclaimed Vanessa, slapping the back of her neck. "Didn't Monoculus say that solving these puzzles would give us a magic word? This is just another math puzzle like the ones we've done already."

Alex scratched his ankle. "He said that if we add up all the results, we would get the magic word."

"How do we squeeze a word out of this stuff?" asked Sam, pulling the hood of his sweatshirt tighter around his head. "Do you think the numbers will turn into letters just like that?"

"Why not?" replied Alex. "We've seen some pretty amazing things so far."

"Okay. Let's hope you're right," said Sam and returned to the fish puzzle. "So, before the meal each fish weighs three times as much as the one just below it. And the biggest one weighs 162 kilos until it gobbles up the rest. We have to figure out the weights of all the fish before the meal, and then add that to 162."

"If the biggest fish is three times heavier than the second-biggest fish, 162 must be divisible by 3," said Vanessa. She scribbled for a moment. "Yup, it's 54. The second-biggest first weighs 54 kilos."

Sam picked it up from there. "Then we divide 54 by 3 to get the weight of the middle fish. Um . . . 18 kilos."

"Ow! I think that was a blackfly!" exclaimed Alex, clapping his hand to his ear. "Okay, 18 kilos divided by 3 is 6. So 6 kilos is how much the second-smallest fish weighs. And 6 divided by 3 is 2. Therefore, the smallest fish weighs 2 kilos."

Sam continued: "So let's take all these weights and add them up: $2 + 6 + 18 + 54 + 162 = 242$. The biggest fish weighs 242 kilos after the meal. Done!"

"That wasn't too hard," said Vanessa. "But I'd like it even more if we had Alex's desk instead of this stump to work on. And the bugs are driving me crazy."

"Yeah, but this is kind of neat," said Sam. "We solve puzzles and get a free adventure thrown in. Plus, a bonus sailing period!"

"Anything for a chance to sail, eh?" laughed Alex. "Well, there's always The Cave. I'm sure no mosquitoes would dare follow us in there."

There was a moment of silence, then Alex said, "Uh, I'm joking, guys."

Sam let out a sigh of relief. Practically every night at campfire they were terrified by a story about the cave on Blackwell Island. Sometimes someone was murdered there; other times a miner or spelunker was lost in the cave's mysterious depths. One story had been about a hermit who lived there and went crazy; another about a vampire and his flock of vampire bats. Whatever the story, it always ended with some foolish camper or another entering the cave and coming out gibbering – or not coming out at all. There was no mosquito alive that could send Alex, Sam or Vanessa into that cave, no way.

"Snack time," said Vanessa, and that broke the scary mood. Sam had been eyeing the chocolate bars and did not wait to be asked twice. The food vanished so quickly, one might have suspected magic. Feeling very satisfied, the kids listened to the sounds of the forest and were already beginning to grow used to it all when suddenly the bushes behind them began to rustle. They barely had a moment to turn around when a large shape appeared out of the shadows.

"It's Rechner!" cried out Sam, and dropped his juice bottle.

Alex was fumbling with his flashlight which had suddenly gone out, while Vanessa grabbed the book and was trying to hide it behind the stump.

When Alex finally got the flashlight working again, the deepest sigh of relief in the history of Blackwell Island was heaved by three pairs of lungs. The curious brown eyes of a deer were staring at the children, but only for a moment. As soon as the beam of Alex's flashlight strafed the animal's head, the intruder was gone as quickly as it had appeared.

"I thought you said no one lived on this island," whispered Vanessa's quivering voice.

"Deer don't count," Sam whispered back, in only a slightly stronger voice, and picked up *Jayden's Rescue* from the ground. "Besides, they probably don't actually live here. They just swim over once in a while."

Although everyone was quite shaken, there was work to be done and little time left to do it in. The next puzzle was strangely appropriate.

At midnight sharp two goblin friends
will start a goblin dance.
Under the moon, among the trees,
the goblins love to prance!
At five past twelve, these goblins leave,
so four can take their place.

At ten past twelve, four must depart,
while eight waltz in with grace.
At quarter past, six dancers flee,
and sixteen join the ball;
Five-minute shifts mark every switch.
They heed a magic call.
This will go on till one o'clock.
So tell me if you might:
at one AM how many will
be there to say good night?

"I think the fish puzzle was better," commented Alex, the deer utterly forgotten.

"I like this one," said Vanessa. "Dancing goblins coming and going — sounds like a wild party."

"So, this pattern keeps up until one o'clock," said Sam. "How many five-minute segments are there in an hour?"

"Twelve," said Alex.

"Sixty minutes in an hour; 60 divided by 5 is 12," agreed Sam. He looked curiously at Alex. "How'd you get that so fast?"

"A clock face popped into my mind," said Alex. "You know, the numbers 1 to 12. They're hours to the hour hand, but to the minute hand, they're five-minute intervals."

"Of course. Good one, Alex," said Vanessa. "But isn't this a pattern puzzle as well?

"If it is, I don't see the pattern," said Alex. "2, 4, 8, 6, 16 . . . it doesn't make sense."

"Actually, there are two patterns, one for goblins leaving and one for goblins arriving," said Sam. "And look — the number of arrivals doubles each time."

"But the number of goblins leaving at each switch increases by only two," said Vanessa. "That *is* a wild party. There are way more goblins coming than going!"

"I think we're going to need a chart," said Sam.

Time	Goblins leaving	Goblins arriving
12:05	2	4
12:10	4	8
12:15	6	16
12:20	8	32
12:25	10	64
12:30	12	128
12:35	14	256
12:40	16	512
12:45	18	1,024
12:50	20	2,048
12:55	22	4,096
1:00	24	8,192

"The last step is easy," concluded Vanessa. "We just add up each column, subtract the departure total from the arrival total, and the difference is how many goblins remain to say 'good night' at one o'clock."

"Right," agreed Sam. He got busy with the adding, but Alex was troubled.

"What's the matter?" asked Vanessa.

"Some of the goblins came *and* went, didn't they? Like those two at midnight who started it all! What about them?"

Alex's old math-test panic was starting to hit him. He couldn't see what Sam and Vanessa seemed to see so clearly, and he couldn't explain why. He just didn't get it – he'd never get it!

Vanessa looked thoughtfully at Alex's anxious face. "Well, how would *you* carry on?"

Vanessa's tone of voice had a calming affect. Alex took a deep breath.

"Well, um, I guess I'd start with the two original goblins, add the four that came at 12:05, then subtract the two that left at the same time. Then I'd add eight, and subtract four, and so on."

"Hmmm . . . " said Vanessa. "Well, that seems logical, even if it might take longer."

In short order Sam was done. "At one o'clock, 16,224 goblins said goodnight," he announced.

"I'm going to try your method, Alex," said Vanessa. "Let's see, two goblins, plus four at 12:05, minus two, plus eight at 12:10 . . . " She scribbled away for a while, then cried, "Hey! The answer's different!" She showed Sam and Alex the result: 16,226.

"We'd better check the puzzle again," sighed Sam.

Vanessa started reading aloud. "'At midnight sharp two goblin friends . . . ' oh!" Across the top of the three columns in their chart, she scribbled 12:00, 0 and 2. "Do your stuff, Sam," she said. "We have to be sure it's right."

Sam groaned, but went to work.

"We went off track at the beginning," Vanessa began, then yawned until her jaw cracked. "There were thirteen switches, after all. Good thing you flipped, Alex – your instincts were right on!" She yawned again, and this time, Alex did, too.

Finally Sam was done. "16,226!" he announced. "Alex, I've got to hand it to – " Now it was his turn for the yawn. When he was done, he looked at his watch. "I think we've done enough for tonight. If we leave now, we'll get at least half a night of sleep."

The kids picked up their things and headed back toward the lake. But when they arrived at the cove, the boat was not there.

"What next?" exclaimed Vanessa. "Now we're really in for it."

"I thought you knew special sailors' knots, Sam," said Alex reproachfully.

"I tied a perfect knot!" replied Sam, clearly offended. "Look. The log isn't there either. It must have been loose to begin with."

Alex began to scour the waters with his flashlight, and sure enough, the light bounced off a green object slowly drifting about twenty metres off shore.

"There's the boat, and it's still attached to the log!" shouted Sam. "I told you my knot was good!"

"One of us will have to swim for it," said Vanessa. "And it can't be me: I wouldn't know what to do with the sail once I got there."

"Neither would I," said Alex. "Besides, I don't feel much like swimming after what happened yesterday."

Sam did not look eager to get wet either. The water seemed pretty cold in the middle of the night. But there was no choice. "Shine your flashlights in front of me, then. And if you think I'll enjoy this, I won't," said Sam. And he stepped into the lake.

It didn't take long for Sam to reach the boat. Alex and Vanessa watched him in suspense as he heaved himself aboard and began to prepare everything. Once the sail was in place, Sam untied his expert knot, waved goodbye to the log and headed back to the island. The others climbed in, and they crossed the lake back to camp. They really appreciated having a craft that made no noise as they glided in place at the dock.

As soon as the boat was locked up, the kids raced through the woods toward Vanessa's cabin. After dropping her off, the boys made it back to their own cabin and snuck in without waking anyone. For the remainder of the night they all slept more soundly than Sleeping Beauty herself.

Chapter 10

Reversal of Fortune

In the morning everyone was up except for Alex and Sam. Vanessa was also still in bed when all the girls in her cabin were rolling up their sleeping bags and getting ready for breakfast. But in the end the three conspirators did meet in the lineup for porridge. Yawning and stretching, Alex, Sam and Vanessa finished eating and left the mess hall with little desire to do anything but go back to sleep. However, Alex and Sam had already signed up for basketball and were expected to be there. Vanessa had tennis.

Throughout the day, keeping their minds on what they were doing was no mean task. The basketball game was a disaster. Sam did not score a single point, and

Alex kept passing the ball to the other team. At tennis Vanessa served into the net every time, making her doubles partner livid. Then, at the pottery workshop, Sam created an elegant bowl — or at least what might have been a bowl, until the wheel spun out of control. The clay ended up splattered all over the ceiling and the face of a kid called Harry who was from the same cabin as Alex and Sam. For the rest of the session Harry eyed Sam with great suspicion.

As soon as Alex lay down on his bunk at lights-out, he fell asleep, even though he had promised to stay up. Sam had to wake him shortly before eleven, shaking him several times and whispering in his ear. Vanessa was also barely able to crawl out of bed. But they did manage to get to the dock and sail to the island without any problems. This time they tied the boat to a strong willow tree right by the water's edge and headed for their puzzle stump. Now they had insect repellent, which made a big difference.

Yawning like a hippopotamus, Alex said, "I wonder if we can face any more puzzles in this shape."

"We'll do as much as we can," said Vanessa, "and then why don't we skip tomorrow night. If we don't get more sleep, we won't be able to solve anything."

Alex and Sam agreed. They opened the book and saw the third puzzle:

A stock of oatmeal cookies filled Megan's pantry shelves.
At midnight cookie raiders snuck in and helped themselves.
The cookies were so crunchy! The thieves adored their taste.
A fifth of all the cookies were swallowed in great haste.
The ones uneaten numbered one hundred thirty-two.

Who could have done this evil? Meg did not have a clue.
She called a nice policeman who saw she was distressed;
He asked how many cookies the victim once possessed.
But Meg could not remember, and so we ask of you:
Please help her with the answer, or Meg will cry, boo-hoo!

"Cookies!" exclaimed Alex. "Just what I'd like to get my hands on right now."

"You'll get a cookie as soon as we solve this one," said Vanessa. "I just happened to get some in a parcel from my parents."

"Are they oatmeal?" asked Alex hopefully.

"Sorry, chocolate chip," said Vanessa.

"Chocolate chip!" exclaimed Sam. "Better than oatmeal any day. Okay, back to Meg and her troubles. Meg has an unknown total before the raid and loses 1/5. 132 cookies are left. To figure out 1/5, all we have to do is divide 132 by 5. Then . . . "

"Not so fast, Captain Chocolate Chip," interrupted Vanessa. "That would give us 1/5 of 132. But it was 1/5 of the total that the cookie raiders took, and that left 132. Right?"

"Oh yeah!" agreed Sam and wrinkled his brow.

"1/5 goes into the total five times," said Vanessa. "If you take away 1/5, there are 4/5 left. 132 amounts to 4/5. That means four equal parts."

"So all we have to do is figure out the four equal parts that go into 132," said Sam. "132 divided by 4 makes 33."

"And now, presto!" exclaimed Alex standing up and making magical movements with his hands. "Add the 4/5, that is 132, and the 1/5, that is 33. What you get is . . . ala-kazam: 165! That's how many cookies Meg had before the raid." Alex took a bow in every direction. Sam and Vanessa clapped, laughing like monkeys.

"Cookie time!" remembered Sam and dove into Vanessa's knapsack. Now the quiet of the night was broken only by hungry crunching. Then an owl hooted somewhere in the trees above. This time no one even flinched. A moment later the huge bird took off and flew away grace-fully toward the camp. For a second, while the bird was still close to the ground, its huge wingspan seemed to cover half of the night sky. It was the first time they had ever seen a live owl.

"Doesn't this beat sitting in my room?" whispered Alex as he brushed the last crumbs of cookie off his pants.

"I can stay awake for one more puzzle . . . maybe," sighed Vanessa and yawned so enticingly that the other two could not help but yawn and stretch in response. They closed the book again and opened it as they had done so many times before. Monoculus's fourth puzzle was there as expected. But it was not nearly as appetizing as the previous one.

Three happy worms loved apples most and ate them from inside.
They had a way of getting in despite the pesticide.
The smallest one could eat, per day, ten grams of apple pulp.
The middle one would skip a day, and thirty grams could gulp.
The biggest one would wait two days; then fifty grams were gone.
And so it went, from dawn to dusk and then from dusk to dawn.
Eight apples, eighty grams apiece, were hanging on their tree.

How long, I wonder, did they last among those wiggly three?
(And I must add that on day one each worm began to chew,
For they were hungry and did not have better things to do.)

"Yuck," said Vanessa, making a face. "It's a good thing we've already had our snack."

"So the first worm eats 10 grams every day, the second eats 30 grams every other day and the third eats 50 grams every third day," said Sam. "They polish off 8 apples, and each apple weighs 80 grams. Hmm . . . this is tricky."

"Well, at least we can start by figuring out how many grams they ate all together," said Alex. "8 apples times 80 grams would equal 640 grams."

"Let's make another chart," proposed Vanessa. "All three worms begin eating on Day 1:"

	Worm 1	Worm 2	Worm 3
Day 1	10 grams	30 grams	50 grams
Day 2	10 grams	—	—
Day 3	10 grams	30 grams	—
Day 4	10 grams	—	50 grams
Day 5	10 grams	30 grams	—
Day 6	10 grams	—	—
Day 7	10 grams	30 grams	50 grams
Day 8	10 grams	—	—

"Okay, that's enough for now," suggested Alex. "How many grams of apple does this make?"

"350," replied Sam after a quick calculation. "Let's keep going."

Day 9	10 grams	30 grams	—
Day 10	10 grams	—	50 grams
Day 11	10 grams	30 grams	—
Day 12	10 grams	—	—
Day 13	10 grams	30 grams	50 grams
Day 14	10 grams	—	—
Day 15	10 grams	30 grams	—

Total: 150 grams + 240 grams + 250 grams
= 640 grams (8 eighty-gram apples)

"Fifteen days," said Vanessa. "I feel like I've been awake that long. That's it. I can't stay up any more."

"Back to the boat," agreed Sam and put the book into Alex's knapsack. Fortunately this time the boat was where they'd left it. They pushed off and headed for camp, thinking only of their comfy sleeping bags.

The following morning, waking up was even harder than before. They had trouble doing their activities again, and after going swimming, all three fell asleep right on their beach towels in the shade of a tree. However, that didn't last long because Harry and some other kids poured a bucket of water on their backs and ran away giggling. At nine o'clock that night, Alex, Sam and Vanessa did not hear the lights-out signal; they were already "out" on their bunks. Finally, a whole, wonderful night of sleep.

On the morning of the fourth day after Rechner's appearance by the ski dock, Alex, Vanessa and Sam had to take stock of the situation and figure out how to divide up the remaining time.

"We have four nights left and three puzzles to do," Vanessa began. "We should have no problem."

"But I don't think I can take two sleepless nights in a row again," objected Sam. "We'll have to finish everything tonight."

"Well, we can try," agreed Vanessa. "Let's set our brains to full capacity. We'll need lots of snacks, and I think it's your turn to pop into the tuck shop."

Once again that night they were quietly making their way down an already familiar path toward the lake. Alex stopped for a second to take a pebble out of his shoe. "I'll catch up to you," he whispered. "Keep going."

While he was busy with his shoelaces, Alex suddenly heard voices and saw beams of light.

"What are you two doing out here so late? What cabins are you from? Don't you know it's not allowed? Come on. We'll escort you back. Your counsellors will have to hear about this."

Oh no! The patrol! Alex had not been seen, but Sam and Vanessa were now heading back in his direction, accompanied by two rather irate counsellors. What rotten luck! Alex cowered behind a bush, watching his friends pass right in front of his nose. Vanessa noticed Alex's pale face amongst the leaves and gave him a parting, almost hopeless glance.

Then he heard something drop on the path. When the coast was clear, he shone his flashlight on the ground and saw . . . Vanessa's knapsack, and a small, shiny object next to it. The padlock key!

Alex picked up the key and the knapsack, not knowing

what he was going to do. For a moment fear was all he felt. Turning back seemed like a really good idea. But Alex was sure that after this incident, the patrols would be keeping an eye on their cabins. So this was the last chance. It was now or never.

The last hope of the Emerald Queen and her rescue team rested with him.

Chapter 11

The Last Stretch

Alex put the key in his pocket, swung Vanessa's knapsack over his left shoulder, and, with his own knapsack on his right shoulder, rushed down the path.

When he arrived at the dock, he unlocked the padlock and started to reconstruct Sam's movements in his mind. When he tried to copy them, amazingly, it all fell into place. He remembered where the sails went and even figured out the rigging. Great. Now what? He jumped into the boat and pushed off.

At first everything seemed fine, but then he noticed that the boat was wheeling around and heading back toward camp. Twice Alex made large circles on the water, unable to find a way of getting the boat to obey. All the time he was struggling, he dreaded the patrol catching sight of the boat in the lagoon. Finally, the rudder did its job, and the boom swung into position. He rounded the point without mishap and the island was straight ahead. Please don't let anything happen! Please! he begged silently.

It was not a totally smooth landing, but there he was, in the cove. He tied the boat to the familiar willow tree, hoping ordinary knots would do. Alex soon found himself on solid ground, slightly shaken, but in one piece. He looked around and felt very small under the gathering clouds that were slowly obstructing the full moon. He was all alone on an isolated island.

Alex took a deep breath. Keep calm, you can do it! he told himself. He pointed his flashlight outward like a sword and started moving inland on unsteady legs. There was the familiar stump. Nothing had changed, except that Sam and Vanessa were on the other side of the lake. They were probably lying awake in their cabins, worrying about what he was doing. Perhaps Sam was thinking that Alex would never be able to set up the sails, let alone sail to the island by himself. Boy, would he be surprised!

Thinking about his friends made Alex feel even more alone. Then Alex remembered: Monoculus. He was not alone after all. Alex eagerly opened the book and saw Monoculus's reassuring face. And there was the fifth puzzle:

A jolly, juicy jumping bug was sauntering along
A praying mantis lunged at him and wished to do him wrong.
The bug fled fast. He huffed and puffed. His speed was hard to beat.
One hundred centimetres flat per second — what a feat!

The hunter's speed was not a joke; impressive was his gait.
Per minute thirty metres is a very daunting rate.
Pray, do not keep me in suspense and tell me, I implore,
If at the end the mantis was as hungry as before.
In centimetres, if you please, per second, I might add,
What was the difference in their speeds? Good hunting to you, lad.

A praying mantis? A jumping bug? Alex looked up at the sky. It was as dark as before. The wind made the tree-tops sway like huge fans. Forest noises came from all around him. Maybe there were praying mantises hunting juicy bugs on this very island.

Concentrate, concentrate, Alex reminded himself. The bug's speed was given in centimetres per second, but the praying mantis's was in metres per minute. Alex realized that he had to compare apples to apples here (without worms, he thought with a smile). The bug's speed and the praying mantis's speed had to be measured the same way. That was when he remembered the table of weights and measures inside Vanessa's knapsack. Thank you, Vanessa!

He looked up centimetres on the little card. 100 centimetres in a metre. So, he thought, picking up his pencil,

The bug runs at 100 cm per second. The praying mantis's speed is 30 m per minute. That means the praying mantis's speed is 30 x 100 = 3000 cm per minute.

The praying mantis moves at 3000 cm per minute. There are 60 seconds in a minute. The praying mantis's speed per second is:

3000 divided by 60 = 50.

The praying mantis runs at 50 cm per second. The bug runs at 100 cm per second. The difference between their speeds is 100 − 50 = 50 cm per second.

The bug ran at double the praying mantis's speed! It was safe, and the mantis was hungry. So was Alex. He dug into the food he and Sam had picked up at the tuck shop.

Munching on a fruit bar, Alex thought that nothing could get in his way now . . . except for the drops that he suddenly felt on his head. Quickly swallowing the last bite, Alex grabbed all his things and ran for cover under a pine tree. The rain began to come down hard, threatening to ruin everything. *Jayden's Rescue* had to be protected at all costs. He stashed the book, as well as all the notes, in his knapsack and looked at the dismal sky. There was no sign that this would be just a passing shower.

Alex knew of only one sheltered place on Blackwell Island. He weighed the options. He could risk The Cave, on the off chance that all the campfire stories had been only that, stories. Or, he could give up now and risk being put into Rechner's dungeon.

Well, Alex had seen the dungeon, and he wasn't keen to live there, much less drag his best friends in. He rushed out from under his tree and fled down a narrow path toward the middle of the island. For quite a while his flashlight revealed nothing but trees and bushes in every direction. Then he noticed a large dark mass in the distance and stopped. Alex had found what he was looking for.

Alex might still have hesitated before going inside the cave, but the rain turned into a downpour and drove him on. Drenched to the bone, he dashed into the dark opening in the rock.

He found himself in a cozy enclosure. There were no bats, and if there were any ghosts, then they must have been away scaring campers on the mainland. Alex placed his flashlight upright, creating a reflection against the ceiling of the cave. Too bad they hadn't found this great spot right from the beginning.

Only two more puzzles were left. Alex opened the book and saw that Monoculus was ready with puzzle number six. It was a really short one this time. Short meant easy . . . right?

I have a little sister. Her age is eighty-four.
I recently turned ninety, a fact that I deplore!
When we were so much younger, I was three times her age.
How old was I? Go figure, and be like me, a sage.

This was the second time that Monoculus had come up with a puzzle about himself. Now Alex knew his age and that he had a younger sister as well as all those one-eyed sons. This somehow made the monster seem even more real than before.

Alex read the puzzle several times and began to suspect that there was some kind of mistake. Monoculus at age 90 wasn't much older than his 84-year-old sister. How could he have ever been three times her age?! If only Vanessa and Sam were here! Alex got up and walked around the cave to clear his mind. Then he looked outside. It was still raining cats and dogs.

He returned to the puzzle and considered what he knew. He knew that Monoculus was three times his sister's age a long time ago, because they were "so much younger." He also knew that the difference between their ages was six years; $90 - 84 = 6$. Then he remembered the lock puzzle on the back cover of *Jayden's Rescue*. As the magic pencil was doing the first part of the solution, it used the letters X and Y for unknown numbers. Maybe that was the way to go . . . Alex started to write:

> The sister's age when they were younger is X.
> Monoculus's age when they were younger is Y.
> $3 \times X = Y$

Hmm . . . but Monoculus was also six years older than his sister. Alex wrote,

> $6 + X = Y$

Then he wrote,

> $6 + X = 3 \times X$

Now that was an interesting-looking equation. But it still wasn't enough to go on. Alex would have to plug in numbers the way they had done with the lock puzzle. He might as well start with 1.

$$6 + 1 = 7 \qquad 6 + 2 = 8 \qquad 6 + 3 = 9$$
$$3 \times 1 = 3 \qquad 3 \times 2 = 6 \qquad 3 \times 3 = 9$$

$$6 + 3 = 3 \times 3$$

That was it! Y, or Monoculus's age, was nine! And X, the sister's age, was three. Wait till Sam and Vanessa heard about this one!

But there was no time for patting himself on the back. Another snack and back to work. It was time for the last puzzle.

> *Three hundred seats in equal rows*
> *will fill a roomy hall.*
> *A film of wonder will be shown*
> *to children, big and small.*
> *Two hundred forty children come*
> *which leaves some empty rows.*
> *How many rows are left untouched?*
> *Please ponder and disclose.*
> *Half of the seats per vacant row,*
> *if multiplied by four,*
> *would equal all the empty seats.*
> *That's all. Oh, one thing more:*
> *The screen is where your troubles end.*
> *So watch and don't despair.*
> *When you have seen the mist, my friends,*
> *you'll know that you are there.*

Alex nervously licked his lips. There was more than just

a puzzle here. The first part made sense, but what about the last two lines? What mist? What was the connection? Alex spent some time trying to make the link, but no matter how much he reread the whole puzzle, nothing came to mind. In the end he decided to leave it for the time being and busied himself with figuring out how many rows would be left vacant in the roomy hall. It occurred to him that he could begin with the difference between all the available seats and the occupied ones: $300 - 240 = 60$. Then Alex went on, writing as he thought.

> The rows are all equal. The number of seats per row is X. $X \div 2$ is half a row. That number multiplied by 4 equals 60 (all the empty seats). So $(X \div 2) \times 4 = 60$.

Alex paused and stared at his last equation for a while. Something times 4 equalled 60. Didn't that mean that 60 divided by 4 equalled something? Multiplication and division were related, after all.

Alex wrote on:

> $(X \div 2) \times 4 = 60$ in reverse is $60 \div 4 = X \div 2$
> $60 \div 4 = 15$, so $X \div 2 = 15$
> This in reverse is $15 \times 2 = 30$
> So $X = 30$. Each row has 30 seats.

Alex had the number of seats per row, but he needed the number of empty rows. He looked at the puzzle again. The total number of empty seats was sixty, and 30 went into

60 twice. That meant there were two empty rows in the hall.

As soon as Alex had written the answer down, he glanced at the book. The expression on Monoculus's face had changed even while the book had been left open. The monster looked overjoyed. The last two mysterious lines of the puzzle still bothered Alex, but Monoculus's new expression reassured him. Seven puzzles had been solved!

And now for the big moment: all the results from the puzzles had to be added up. Would the final number somehow turn into a word, as Alex had imagined? He went through all the island notes and wrote down the answer for each puzzle on a new sheet of paper. Then he began to add.

Fish:	242
Goblins:	16,226
Cookies:	165
Days:	15
Centimetres/second:	50
Age:	9
Rows:	2
	————
Total:	16,709

Immediately after writing the total, Alex closed his eyes. When he opened them, he was disappointed. The number was still just a number. He closed his eyes again. Then he tried walking away and coming back. No word appeared. Alex tried the old trick of opening and closing the book several times, hoping Monoculus would offer more advice, but he did not. In fact, when Alex looked at Monoculus closely, he was amazed to see that the monster's only eye was closed. He was asleep! Even one-eyed monsters get tired, Alex guessed.

The rain had now slowed to a drizzle. With nothing else left to do, Alex gathered up all his things and trudged along the muddy path all the way back to the cove. The boat was full of water and barely floated above the surface, so bailing it out took a long time. As Alex worked, he kept muttering 16,709, 16,709, 16,709 . . .

Finally, the boat was ready, and Alex glumly set sail for Camp Waconda. A light fog had lifted over the lake, concealing Alex's return to the sailing dock as dawn slowly made its cheerful presence known.

He returned to his cabin only to find that Rick was awake and furious. With the coming of morning the stuff in his bed had been discovered. When Alex walked in the counsellor exploded.

"Taking walks in the middle of the night, are you?" he barked. "What do you think you're doing? Where were you? When Jeff finds out, you'll be sent home for sure! Now go to bed."

Alex said nothing, clutching the two knapsacks and shivering. As he changed into his pajamas, he was itching to tell Sam about everything that had happened. But for the time being this had to wait.

During free time that afternoon Sam, Alex and Vanessa appeared before Jeff at the office. Surprisingly, Jeff was pretty nice about the whole thing. He didn't even punish them. But he did say that if they were ever again found wandering in the woods after lights-out, their parents would have to be told. And that was it.

As they headed out of the office, Sam and Vanessa were beside themselves with curiosity. There were only fifteen minutes of free time left so Alex had to talk fast to answer all their questions. When they heard about The Cave, their jaws dropped.

"I tell you, it was great," said Alex, enjoying their amazement. "Dry, cozy – really nice."

"No bats, even?" asked Sam, who sounded slightly disappointed.

"Not a single one," Alex assured him.

"And what about the solutions?" asked Vanessa, suddenly remembering the point of it all. "Did you get them? Did they add up to anything?"

"Well," said Alex, "it's like that old joke. I've got some good news and some bad news. Which do you want first?"

"Let's hear the good," said Sam.

"I solved the three remaining puzzles," said Alex proudly.

"All right!" said Vanessa. "And the bad news?"

"I added up all the solutions and got a number – 16,709. But that's all."

They were at the steps of Alex and Sam's cabin now, so Alex went in, brought out his notes and showed them the solutions for puzzles five, six and seven. Then he opened the book to show them Monoculus's last puzzle. As before, Monoculus was fast asleep, which did not make Sam and Vanessa happy. And when they saw the last two lines of the movie puzzle, they were just as perplexed as Alex.

"This bit about despair and the mist doesn't even seem

to be part of the puzzle," observed Vanessa. "What on earth could it mean?"

"I've been thinking about it since last night," replied Alex. "But for now all we have is 16,709. And I still don't have a clue how to turn it into a word."

"There must be a way out of this," said Sam who looked irritated and exhausted. "We can't come this close and fail in the end. Monoculus wouldn't do that to us!"

"Hey," exclaimed Vanessa, "I think I know what's going on. I've seen this before, in a book about a French prisoner. He figures out a way of communicating with the person in the next cell by knocking on the wall. The number of knocks stands for a letter in the alphabet. So number one would be the first letter, A. And so on. They spell words, sentences and then come up with an escape plan. It was such a great story, by Alexandre – "

"Okay, okay," Alex interrupted. "Ours can be a great story too, if we get out of it in one piece." He took out some paper and a pencil.

"Here we go again," groaned Sam.

Alex ignored him. "Let's try to spell 16,709," he said. Quickly, he wrote out the alphabet and assigned each letter a number. "Now, 1 = A; 6 = F; 7 = G . . . "

"But that's where it all falls apart," interrupted Sam in dismay. "The next number is zero. So what letter does that stand for?"

"Just go on," Vanessa said, trying to sound positive. "A, F, G, blank, I."

"What kind of a word is that?" said Sam.

"Hey," suddenly Alex cried out, "the zero could be an O!"

"So is the magic word AFGOI, then?" wondered Vanessa. None of them looked very sure. What if they had it wrong? Things were definitely not turning out to be as neat as expected.

"Well, AFGOI it'll have to be," said Alex. "That's all we have. I just hope it'll put Rechner away . . . "

Chapter 12

The Magic Word

The night before Rechner was supposed to return, Sam, Vanessa and Alex headed reluctantly to the auditorium. Once in a while Jeff would organize something for everyone in the big hall. A week earlier, a group of children's entertainers had been invited, and before that, a woman had brought in all kinds of snakes, fish, salamanders, frogs and lizards to show the campers. No one knew what kind of special event was about to take place, but the camp was abuzz with excitement. Only three kids were not looking forward to the upcoming surprise.

"Maybe we should get rid of the book," suggested Sam. "If we destroy it, the castle will be gone. Rechner can't imprison us in a castle that doesn't exist, can he? Besides, it would be the end of Rechner too."

"But what about Monoculus?" asked Vanessa. "He would also be destroyed."

"You're right," said Sam. Then after a few moments he went on, "I have an idea: why don't we call our parents and tell them to come take us home? We'll say we're homesick."

"But Rechner is coming back tomorrow," objected Vanessa. "Our parents couldn't get us out of here that fast. And Rechner would probably come after us wherever we were."

They walked into the auditorium and looked around. Everyone was crowded at the front as some seats at the back were roped off, and it was hard to find three chairs side by side. But Sam spotted some, and they sat down.

"Hello, my fellow Wacondians," said Jeff as soon as everyone had settled into their seats. "I know you'd rather be out there feeding the mosquitoes, but I thought you might want to take a little break from that noble activity and watch . . . a movie!"

A roar of approval greeted the director's announcement, and it took Jeff a little while to make himself heard again.

"Today's feature is a thrilling ride into the depths of suspense and . . . meteorology, and what this blockbuster is called is . . . " Jeff fumbled with a piece of paper and then read out loud: "*The Endless Sea.*"

Even though the title hardly sounded familiar, the audience did not lose its enthusiasm, and everyone stared at the screen with great interest.

As Alex scanned the animated faces of all the other campers, his expression changed. He gestured wildly toward the back of the room and hissed, "Do you see what I see?"

Sam and Vanessa looked where their friend was pointing, then back at Alex with puzzlement in their faces.

"Ness, Sam! Open your eyes! There are two empty rows!" Alex stood up. "I have to count all the seats," he muttered.

"What are you going on about?" asked Vanessa, looking completely lost.

"You'll see in a moment," said Alex as he counted the seats in one row. "Just as I thought: thirty seats per row. Now how many rows? Ten! 30 times 10 is 300. There are 300 seats here and two rows of thirty are empty! Wow!"

"He's finally cracked," said Sam to Vanessa. "See? There is something about The Cave!"

"Oh no!" said Alex. "I'm as sharp as ever. This is just like the seventh puzzle. The auditorium is our 'roomy hall!' Remember the strange ending? 'The screen is where your troubles end. So watch and don't despair.' We're in despair, and a movie is about to start. Our troubles will be solved on the screen!"

Sam and Vanessa stared at Alex as their confusion turned into jubilation, then admiration, then awe.

"Al, you are the greatest puzzle sleuth of all times!" uttered Sam breathlessly.

"I guess we get to enjoy the film after all," said Vanessa

and made herself comfortable. The lights were dimmed and the movie began.

It was an adventure story about three fishermen who go out to sea and end up caught in a thick fog. For days they drift, slowly exhausting their food and water supplies. Unable to determine where the shoreline is, they keep hoping that the fog will lift sooner or later. But nothing changes, and they realize that they are about to face terrible thirst and hunger.

Once their little boat is almost overturned by a sea creature; another time an ocean liner passes within a few metres of them. But no one on board can hear the fishermen's cries, and the ship sails away. After many other adventures and close calls, in utter despair, the three men are saved by a school of dolphins which seem to understand the situation, and guide the boat to shore.

"That's *it?*" said Sam, as the film credits rolled and the lights were switched back on.

"I don't think any dolphins are going to help the three of *us*," sighed Alex.

Gone was their previous optimism. Trudging along a dark path toward their cabins, they considered the situation.

"The movie did not give us a clue," said Sam, shaking his head. "Monoculus let us down. And tomorrow we have to face the music."

"Well, we do have this AFGOI word," replied Vanessa. "What if it's the magic word after all? I'll bet Monoculus will come through in the end." She did not sound very convinced.

"Look," said Alex, "remember what Monoculus told us a week ago after Rechner had snapped my tow rope? 'If a secret word is spoken right to Rechner's wicked face, Rechner will be locked forever in this godforsaken place.' That means Rechner's castle, and the castle is in the book. So tomorrow we have to take the book down to the ski dock, wait for Rechner to appear, say AFGOI to him and cross our fingers."

There was nothing else left to say or do now, and soon they parted for the night, Alex and Sam heading to the boys' glen, Vanessa turning toward the girls' side.

Next morning, they skipped breakfast and headed straight for the ski dock. They wanted to be there before all the other kids and counsellors arrived for waterfront activities. Alex had *Jayden's Rescue* tucked away in his backpack.

On the way they passed Ron who was heading uphill back toward the camp.

"Hi, guys! You'll be glad to know that Jeff said water-skiing is on again. And look – I've bought a new tow rope. Do you feel like going out for a spin today, Alex? This time it won't snap, I promise."

"I don't know if I'm into water-skiing anymore, Ron," replied Alex, eyeing the rope in Ron's hands with apprehension.

"Well," said Ron, "let me know if you change your mind. I'll be down again in half an hour. I have to get the motorboat. See you soon."

The air was crisp, and the three shivered as they trod on the sandy beach. The birds were chirping as happily as ever, unaware of what was about to happen at the water's edge in Camp Waconda. When they glimpsed the ski dock, the kids slowed down their pace, expecting to see Rechner any minute. But there were no signs of anything unusual, so they cautiously stepped onto the boards, peering uneasily into the blue-grey water below.

At once everything became still. Even the birds stopped singing. Not the slightest movement of air disturbed the trees or the lake. Alex anxiously glanced up the hill, expecting people would start coming down any moment. But then it happened. The water began to bubble and hiss all around the dock, and the familiar menacing face was before them once again. Rechner's image glared at the children from below without saying a word. He was obviously expecting Jayden to be delivered into his hands.

"Say it, quickly!" whispered Sam to Alex and nudged him toward the edge of the dock.

Alex stood up, took *Jayden's Rescue* out of his backpack with trembling hands and cleared his throat. "AFGOI," he said in a hesitant voice and took a step back, anxiously glancing at Vanessa.

"Say it again, louder," Vanessa prodded. She was as pale as the birch trees behind them.

"AFGOI!" repeated Alex with slightly more force. But Rechner's image only scowled at his victims. His mouth began to open and hideous laughter was heard out of the water. A powerful wind appeared out of nowhere and made the trees sway as if before a thunderstorm. Clouds suddenly covered the sky.

"It's not working! It's the wrong word!" Alex cried out. "What do we do?" The wind seemed to be tearing the book out of his hands, and the waves on the lake were soaking the boards of the ski dock.

Suddenly the water around Rechner's image began to rise slowly toward the children, taking on the sorcerer's shape. Watery arms reached out of the lake.

Frantically, Sam yelled, "Try another letter combination!"

"IOFGA!" screamed Alex at the top of his voice. "GAFIO!" Nothing. Only more laughter and wind.

Now Rechner's shape was above the dock, bending over the kids in an arc of shimmering blue. The sorcerer was becoming huge before their eyes, and his merciless face floated like a mask at the top of the overwhelming figure.

Sam looked utterly helpless, but Vanessa's expression changed abruptly, as if something important had occurred to her. She gasped and turned to Alex.

"The mist! The mist! The clue in the last puzzle!"

"What are you talking about?" replied Alex, almost sobbing now. "I don't understand . . . "

"'Mist' is another word for 'fog'," exclaimed Vanessa and continued so quickly that the others could barely keep up with her. "The movie last night was about three fishermen lost in a fog . . . Don't you get it! Your name: Alex Isaac Fog. A. I. Fog. Rearrange the letters in the magic word and you get AIFOG!"

"Say it, Al!" shouted Sam whose expression changed to absolute glee as the meaning of Vanessa's words sank in. "The word was meant for you all along! Say it to him now!"

Just then, like an avalanche, Rechner rushed down toward the kids from his enormous height. It looked like nothing could stop the bulk that was about to engulf them – but something did.

"AIFOG! AIFOG! AIFOG!" yelled Alex, raising *Jayden's Rescue* high above his head.

"AIFOG! AIFOG!" echoed Sam and Vanessa, screaming the magic word with fury and frenzy. Just a few centimetres short of the children's heads, the sorcerer stopped, and immediately began to shrink back toward the surface of the lake. The kids kept repeating "AIFOG" over and over and the word seemed to hit the sorcerer like blows. Each time they hurled it, Rechner's face shook as if in pain. His formerly triumphant expression changed to one of dismay and then horror, as he finally became once again only a flat image floating by the dock.

And next, the water around Rechner began to turn, spinning faster and faster, as if a whirlpool were forming. The kids were sprayed from head to toe. The gurgling sound coming out of the lake became louder, like a waterfall approaching. Then a shadow zoomed straight up into the air and was sucked into the book through the door in the back cover. Alex's hands shook as if he were holding a madly writhing fire hose. The door shut itself with a thud, there was a click and all was quiet again. Rechner's reflection was gone, and the whirlpool became once again the calm surface of the lake. There was not a trace of wind or clouds left. It was as if nothing had happened.

Alex, Vanessa and Sam looked at the book. The door in the back was not just locked. It was no longer there! The back cover was as smooth as when Alex first saw the book on his shelf, so many weeks ago. And when he tried to open the book, he could not do it. *Jayden's Rescue* was one solid mass.

Alex nervously licked his lips and put the book carefully into the knapsack. Not a word was spoken. The three of them just looked at one other, standing still in the early morning sunshine.

Then the sound of Ron's approaching motorboat broke the spell of the moment. The kids watched as he rode up and tied the boat to the dock. As he jumped out, the kids saw that he was holding out a life jacket.

"I'm ready to ski now," said Alex quietly, and began to take off his shoes.

Epilogue

By the time the first day of school rolled around, Camp Waconda was but a memory – though an unforgettable one. After returning from that incredible vacation, Alex had put *Jayden's Rescue* back on his shelf and gone off to finish the summer. So the subject of his conversation with Sam and Vanessa on the bus was pretty typical.

"I wonder who our new teachers are going to be," said Sam.

"Wouldn't it be great if we all ended up in the same class?" said Vanessa.

"Sure, but that's not going to happen," said Sam. "What are the odds?"

"Well, let's calculate . . . " Alex said with a grin.

"No, let's just cross our fingers, toes, arms and legs," proposed Vanessa, laughing wildly and twisting up like a pretzel.

Suddenly Alex gasped. "Hey!"

Sam and Vanessa crowded close to the window to look where their friend was pointing. On the sidewalk they saw a tall red-headed woman wearing an emerald-green dress that looked like something out of a fairy tale. As the school bus approached, she turned her head and seemed to search the windows. For an instant the children were looking directly into her deep green eyes. Then the bus passed; the woman waved and turned the corner as the children stared after her.

"That couldn't be . . . !" whispered Sam.

"I could almost swear . . . " said Vanessa.

Alex said nothing, but the enormous smile spreading across his face spoke volumes.

About the author

Like Alex, Vladimir Tumanov loved books and reading as a kid – but he wasn't very good at math.

Vladimir grew up in the former Soviet Union, and moved to Canada when he was thirteen years old. He is now a professor of language and literature at the University of Western Ontario. He lives in London, Ontario, with his wife and two kids, Alex and Vanessa.